Lock Down Publications and Ca$h
Presents

I0637418

THA
TAKEOVER 3
Legends Don't Retire:
They Reinvent

Written By
KEITH CHANDLER

First Edition 2025

Printed in the United States of America

This is a work of fiction. Names, characters, places, and incidents either are products of the author's imagination or are used fictitiously. Any similarity to actual events or locales or persons, living or dead, is entirely coincidental.

Lock Down Publications
P.O. Box 944
Stockbridge, GA 30281
www.lockdownpublications.com

Like our page on Facebook: Lock Down Publications
www.facebook.com/lockdownpublications.ldp

Stay Connected with Us!

Text **LOCKDOWN** to 22828 to stay up-to-date with new releases, sneak peaks, contests and more…

Like our page on Facebook:
Lock Down Publications

Join Lock Down Publications/The New Era Reading Group

Visit our website:
www.lockdownpublications.com

Follow us on Instagram:
Lock Down Publications

Email Us: We want to hear from you!

Acknowledgements

First and foremost, all praises are due to the man upstairs: The Creator of the Universe.

Lockdown family, thanks for letting me be a part of the circle. Cash, you recognized something in me and gave me a shot. You pushed me to get my books done in ninety days, and so far, I have made every ninety-day mark. I really need that push, so thanks, bro.

To all my fans and readers, I truly appreciate your support. To all my peoples on lockdown, especially the brothas and sistas that are screaming Indiana.

To get specific, my daughters, Jariah, Kai'Dynn, and Ky'mora, I love y'all and can't wait to get home so we can ball out. I just hope it's not too late to have that tight bond. My brother and his family, I see you building, OG. Love, nigga. My sisters, I love y'all, and I'm happy that y'all on y'all grown woman. Pops and Mom, thank you for having a king like me. I know I have taken you through some things, yet you never turned your back on me, Pops. Mom, you've been one of my biggest supporters. Aunt Tarina, Aunt Shante, Cuz Jakkie and her family, Uncle Fred, Grandma Chandler, Nai'Jai, Brian "Anderson", thank y'all all for the support. Cuz James Bryant "Baby J", thanks for pushing me.

If I forgot about you, I'm sorry, but still send my love. Please write to me, and I will add you to the next book. Help me build my mailing list.

Thanks to _____ from Keith Chandler.

Chapter 1

For it to be Christmas break, Indianapolis International wasn't as packed as they thought it would be. Uno and Nasty parked their rental, popped the trunk, and pulled out their traveling suitcases.

"Why are there so many suitcases?" Punkin asked.

"Yeah, why?" Tay-Tay asked with her hand on her hips.

"Because they contain all our clothes and other shit we need," Nasty said, pushing all their luggage toward the check-in.

On schedule, their flight to Birmingham, Alabama, was airborne and headed south. Uno looked at Punkin and grinned. She and Tay-Tay had been trying to figure out exactly what Uno and Nasty had going on.

A few hours later, Uno felt Punkin shake him awake. Their flight had just landed, and everyone was gathering their things and preparing to exit the plane slowly. Uno followed Nasty toward their suitcases, while the women went to grab the rental they had reserved.

"Damn, it's hot," Punkin said, taking off her sweater.

Putting their suitcases in the trunk of their Bentley rental, they all hopped in, heading to The Valley Hotel.

"So, y'all really not gonna let us know where we're going?" Tay-Tay asked as she stared out of the window at the sunny, bright sky in amazement.

Punkin had never been anywhere in the wintertime, and it wasn't snowing or cold. This was new to her.

"We will be there in a little while, so just relax," Uno said.

Punkin and Tay-Tay both rolled their eyes and sat back.

As Nasty headed to the hotel, he smiled, looking back and seeing the two women lightly snorting.

Uno pulled out his cell phone and sent text messages to the rest of the crew and his family to let them know they'd made it without any trouble. Uno let out a sigh of relief when Nasty pulled up to the hotel. The hotel was beautiful. Thanks to Big Dawg's and Ant's connections, Uno was able to put Punkin's business together, along with the trip.

"We're here, y'all!" Uno smiled as the two girls woke up.

"Where are we?" Tay-Tay asked, stretching and surveying her surroundings.

"The Valley Hotel." Nasty smiled. "We figured since y'all haven't been anywhere that's hot in the winter, we came up with spending Christmas and New Year's in the sun on a beach or something," Nasty said.

Punkin smiled. "Y'all the best, bro, and baby."

While the men checked them into the hotel, the women searched through the different brochures from a nearby table.

"Ready, y'all?" Uno asked, walking up to them at the table.

Punkin kissed Uno on the lips. "I'm all yours, baby!" The minute Punkin walked inside their suite, she was immediately impressed.

"Oh, my God!" she said, throwing her hands up to her mouth as she stared at a huge picture of her and Uno standing tall in the living room with a bow on it. She walked over to the romantic fireplace and lit it up. "Oh, baby, you're so sweet to me!" she said as she grabbed the bouquet of roses from the top. She walked through the rest of the suite to further investigate what Uno did.

Meanwhile, Nasty and Tay-Tay were in their suite, going through the same thing.

"Baby, thank you for bringing me on this trip with you. You're the love of my life, and I know you might not believe me, but you're my first love," Tay-Tay said, kissing and hugging Nasty as they stood in front of the bay window.

By nightfall, Punkin had slipped into a sexy, red lingerie set. Uno had a huge smile on his face as he admired Punkin standing at the foot of the bed in a pair of red, expensive pumps. He walked over to the stereo, put on Marvin Gaye's Greatest Hits, and grabbed two wine glasses and the bottle of Ace of Spades. He grabbed Punkin by the hand and led her up the stairs to an awaiting bubble bath. The two found themselves naked by the time they made it to the tub.

Uno took Punkin's hand and helped her into the bath. He handed her one of the glasses, joined her, and poured their drinks. Punkin downed her wine, set her glass down, and hugged Uno's neck. She affectionately placed her forehead against his, massaging his neck.

Uno lifted her out of the water and set her on the edge, easing in between her legs and kissing her neck. Punkin moaned in ecstasy as Uno's tongue slithered around her body. She jumped when she felt Uno's tongue flick her clit. It seemed like he knew her body better than she did.

"Oh, baby. Damn, you feel so good." Punkin moaned as she rubbed the back of his head as he licked her pussy. "I need to feel you inside me," she said, easing his head from between her legs.

The two stared into each other's eyes for a moment before she turned around, gripped the edge, then backed her ass up against him. He eased up behind her, moved her hair to the side, and started passionately licking her neck, pressing down on her clit from the back. He licked down to her ass cheeks.

Chills shot up Punkin's spine when she felt Uno enter the crack of her ass. After dancing his tongue around her ass, he rose to his feet and slowly eased inside of her. Uno passionately placed kisses on her shoulders, slowly easing in and out of her with nice, long, hard, controllable strokes. By 1 a.m., the two were lying in each other's arms, sleeping like they didn't have a care in the world.

Chapter 2

Laughter and screams filled Uno's mom's house as her family talked, and the kids ran around her living room, playing. Uno's entire family, except for him, was sitting around the house, passing out gifts, when they heard a loud noise coming from outside.

Uno's mom peeked out of the door and stared in disbelief.

"Oh, Lord," she said as she threw her hands over her mouth.

Everyone in the house came and peeked out the door. They all got excited as they rushed out.

Uno's sister, mom, grannies, two aunties, uncle, and all the kids stood on the porch with their hands covering their mouths. There were six brand-new BMW trucks for the grown-ups and tricked-out bikes for the kids. Big Dawg and Ant stood back and nodded their heads, smiling at the trucks with the candy paint and rims.

Their mom was speechless as she stared at the brand-new Bentley SUV. It was the same one she told her boys she wanted a few weeks before. Uno's sister was excited when she hopped behind the wheel of her new car. Then, the family knew why Big Dawg and Ant rented a plane for them to get to the city.

Meanwhile, Uno's mom sat in her brand-new truck, admiring the pink and white Gucci leather interior. She turned up the installed sound system and snapped her fingers to R. Kelly. She looked around and stared at her family and kids with joy in her eyes.

***

"Wow! I can't believe this year is gone already. Today is Christmas, it's sunny outside, and we at The Valley Hotel with the men of our lives. Man, this feel like a *Lifetime* movie," Punkin said to Tay-Tay as they ate while the men went to do something.

"We fucking with men who turn movies into reality," Tay-Tay said.

They got up and set their plans in motion for when the men came back. They had their gifts sitting on the table, waiting for them to walk through the door.

"Hey, baby." Tay-Tay ran up to Nasty when he and Uno walked through the door with a few bags in their hands.

"Here. We want y'all to come and open y'all gifts," Punkin said, handing Uno his first gift.

Uno unwrapped the gift. "I love it," he said, holding up an old Gucci sweat fit.

"Now this one!" Punkin handed him another present.

He opened it and smiled. It was a pair of matching Gucci loafers with the gold Gucci symbol.

"This the last one." She handed him another gift, and Uno opened it up.

"Damn, baby!" was all he could say, taking the Gucci timepiece out of the box. "Where all this money come from?" Uno asked with a crazy look on his face.

"I saved most of the money you been giving me," she said, smiling at him. "All the stones in the watch is VVS. You know I had to grab the best for the best," she said.

"Okay, enough of that. It's my turn," Tay-Tay said, handing Nasty three different boxes.

Nasty opened the first one, which was a necklace with his name spelled out in different colored stones. He smiled because it was the same Cuban link he'd seen a few weeks back. He then opened the next one, which was a watch that matched the necklace. Setting it down, he saved the bigger box for last. When he opened it, it was the same Gucci outfit Punkin had gotten for Uno in a different color.

"Y'all did all this?" Nasty asked, kissing Tay-Tay on the lips.

"It's our turn now. So, what y'all get us?" Punkin asked, rushing toward the suitcase that had a lock on it. Tay-Tay followed suit and did the same thing.

The men sat back and watched the ladies struggle with the suitcases. When they popped the locks on the suitcases, both women's hands went over their mouths.

Inside were matching clothes. Both men went shopping together and decided to buy all the same shit. They had a few Gabriela Hearst Sweaters that ran $2,000 apiece, two Omega watches that cost $5,000 each, and they had Prada and Flower Bomb spray.

When Punkin looked harder, she saw the key on the BMW watch keychain.

"Girl, I got a BMW keychain!" Punkin said, holding it up, surprised.

Tay-Tay rummaged through her suitcase and found the same one. She turned and looked at a smiling Nasty.

"We can't have our women riding in something old. We upgraded y'all to brand-new BMW trucks.

"Oh, baby! Oh, baby!" Punkin screamed while hopping around the room.

"Why y'all stop opening y'all suitcases?" Uno asked, motioning to the other ones.

They walked over and opened another one. When they opened it, they stood there, speechless. Different heels, designer boots, and designer dresses from Gucci, Fendi, Prada, and Dior were inside.

"We not done yet," Nasty said, opening another suitcase for Tay-Tay and pulling out brown, black, white, and burgundy jackets from Ralph Lauren, Nili, IENKI IENKI, and Gucci, along with a couple of scarves.

"We have one last move for y'all," Uno said, handing both women a box.

"Wow!" both said as they opened the gifts, and the diamond Zenith watches blinded them.

***

Back in the city, LR watched his niece's and Nasty's kids run through his apartment.

"I want a baby," LR's female friend Rabbitt said out of nowhere as she lay her head on his shoulder and watched the kids have fun.

"What made you say that? Because we too young," LR said, caught off guard by what Rabbitt said.

"I don't know. Being around your family and having fun with them makes me wanna build my own. What? You don't think we could do it?" she asked.

"Whoa, it's nothing like that. Honestly, I think we would be great parents. It's just, when I have kids, I want it to be with my wife," LR said.

***

Later the night before, Uno, Nasty, Tay-Tay, and Punkin all dressed up extra tight and headed to the picnic spot. The two women looked stunning in their outfits. Punkin wore a white Prada jumpsuit with a plunging V-neckline, whereas Tay-Tay wore a bell-sleeved Zuhair Murad dress, showing off her thick thighs. Uno matched Punkin in a pair of white Prada slacks, and Nasty wore a pair of Gucci slacks. During their meal, the four conversed like they hadn't been around each other in years. The women felt honored that the men shut off their phones so they could enjoy the time they had with the ladies without any interruptions.

Earlier that morning, Uno stepped out and wished Tee and Misty a Merry Christmas, and to make sure they received their gifts on time. After dinner, they all headed over to watch the sunset and were rewarded with sweeping views of the verdant landscape, where they took pictures to show their families.

Chapter 3

The two couples had been enjoying all the fruits the hotel had to offer on the trip. They had formed a bond that couldn't be broken. They were from the same hood, but that trip did something for all four.

"Damn, bro, this week went by so fast. I can't believe it's a new year already," Nasty said, passing Uno the blunt.

"Yeah, I know, but this is going to be our year," Uno said, thinking about his plans.

"These are gonna be memories I will never forget," Nasty said, looking through the pictures on his phone that they took during this trip.

***

Back in the city, LR, Lil' E, Babyface, and Mo-Mo couldn't wait until Uno and Nasty got back from their trip. They had unloaded all their workdays ago, and they were almost finished unloading Uno's and Nasty's as well. Life was great for the family. Business was popping like crazy, and being that they were the only ones in the city with dope, they were charging niggas an arm and a leg. The jump out boys ran into four of their spots late last night, but they stayed on top of their game, so they didn't find shit. Word was it was Red or Beeper who'd sent them.

Meanwhile, some of the unfortunate people in the city were panicking. The dope shortage had niggas' spots getting kicked in. Some of the niggas that only knew how to grind were switching over to the robbery game to stay on top. Even the females were going from hairdos to ponytails.

LR, Lil' E, and Mo-Mo cruised around the city, making stops at different spots while blowing a blunt and concealing their identities behind the tint.

Since the city was dry, a lot of Beeper's and Red's people had been copping work from him. Once they saw the size of their cookies, they jumped ship and let them know they would be copping from them after that.

After finishing the blunt, LR's appetite led him to Butler's to grab something to eat. As usual, on Fridays, Butler's was packed. Harding had everyone out. The minute they walked into Butler's, all eyes were on them. They all had jewelry that received lots of attention as it glistened from the lights. They ordered their food and stood off to the side. Then LR hit Uno up to check on them.

***

Uno was chilling, flipping through channels when his cell phone rang, and he picked it up. "What's up?"

"What's going on up there, bro?" LR asked.

"Man, we really having fun! Bro, this is definitely a spot you wanna bring a female you wanna build with. We've been on mountain biking trails, ziplining, rock climbing, and all kinds of other shit. They have some bad ass women up here, too," he said, looking back to make sure Punkin didn't hear him.

"Damn!" LR said, smiling when a female walked over to their table and handed him her number. Once she was gone, he filled Uno in on what was going on in the city.

When the server brought them their goods, he told Uno he'd hit him back later and hung up. They were so high off the attention that they never noticed Man-Man, Beeper, and his crew standing across the room, mugging them.

"I'm telling you, cuz. You sleeping on them niggas. Them niggas are making moves! Right now, they the only niggas in the city pushing work," Man-Man said, looking at Two-Tall.

Beeper bit the inside of his mouth while looking at LR, Lil' E, and Mo-Mo, who were standing there like they didn't care about shit. Females were coming up to them, giving them hugs and kisses like they were some A-list celebrities. Even the niggas were coming up to them, giving them dap, and telling them to stop by their spots. Man-Man got heated when LR looked over at them.

"Sweet," LR said, smiling.

"Let's get out of here before shit gets ugly," Beeper said.

Everyone stood up and headed out the door.

***

Rabbitt was sitting in bed, arms folded, pouting with an attitude as she watched LR get dressed up for the club.

"I don't see why you got to go out to Tremors. Why can't we bring in the New Year's together somewhere else? Uno, Punkin, Nasty, and Tay-Tay are together somewhere."

LR just looked at her and smirked. "I told you before, I'm going out to connect some dots. I'm trying to get to this bag. Every hustler's gonna be at Tremors tonight, so this is the perfect time for me to build our clientele up," he said, pulling his Polo sweater over his head.

Rabbitt hopped out of bed and threw on her Christian Siriano dress. LR stood there and watched Rabbitt get dressed. When she rushed into the bathroom, he knew he wasn't playing games. He shook his head as he looked at his timepiece. It was going on 11 p.m.

He shook his head as he opened the bathroom door. Rabbitt was standing in front of the mirror, putting on her makeup.

"Okay, baby, you can go out with me," LR said as he kissed her neck.

Rabbitt ignored him. She knew he was running that first-grade game, so she spun around and stared at him dead in the eyes. "Listen, nigga. I'ma let you go out and have your fun with your little hoes, but this gonna run your pockets," she said, then headed back to the bedroom.

***

Tremors was packed. Everybody had on their New Year's best. LR and the entire crew were chilling around the bar with bottles in their hands as far as the eye could see.

"Alright, people, we have twenty minutes left in this year," the DJ announced.

The crowd went wild. The bar was swamped, taking last-minute requests, and not to mention, the bar was handing out free glasses of Champagne, thanks to WSF.

LR was busy, having fun, showing off his new jewelry, and throwing up money to Snoop Dogg's *'Hustle and Ball.'* It looked like money snowed around him and his crew. Females were about to fight each other, trying to pick up the money off the floor, while the niggas stood off, mad. LR just smiled as he watched, then took a hit from his bottle.

"Hello, LR," a thick, dark-skinned female named High-High said after pushing her way through the crowd. "Can I share with you?" she brushed up on him and asked in his ear.

LR looked at her and her crew styling in their skirts, dresses, boots, and heels. "Go 'head."

High-High pushed their way to the bar to get a drink. One by one, his crew picked a girl and put in their bids for the night.

"So why are you here tonight?" High-High asked, sipping from a glass of Cristal.

"Maybe I'm in here trying to find me something to get into for the night." LR shrugged his shoulders.

High-High took another sip from her glass with a smirk on her face. She then sassily walked over, eased in between LR's legs, and whispered something in his ear. The more she talked, the more he grinned. She turned around, boldly flipped her dress up, took his hand, and slid it between her legs, letting him know she didn't have anything on under her dress. High-High moaned as LR fingers played around in her love box.

"We have five more minutes, party people! Five minutes, and the new year is here," the DJ said, hyping the club up more.

High-High pulled her dress down, grabbed LR's hands, then danced through the club as she led him to a corner. LR still had pussy juice on his fingers, so he smelled it to make sure it didn't stink. It had a fresh scent to it, so all games were a go for him.

***

"Oh, Uno! God damn, baby. Damn, this dick feels so good!" Punkin moaned as they made love. "Oh. shit, baby. Make this pussy cum." Punkin elevated her pelvis and moaned.

"Baby, hold it in," he said, then shifted his hips from left to right, hitting another one of her spots. He looked at his watch. "Just give me a few more minutes," he whispered in her ear as he started sensually sucking on her hard nipples.

Punkin dug her nails into his back while he slowly long dicked her. "Oh, baby, it's coming!" she cried out, biting down on her lip.

He bent her legs behind her head. "Thirty seconds. Let's do this shit!" he said, then went full beast mode.

Meanwhile, back at the club, LR was in the corner with his pants halfway down. He guided his dick in and out of High-High's mouth.

"Twenty seconds," the DJ announced. High-High started to pick up the pace, letting LR fuck her mouth while she rubbed on her clit.

Back at the hotel, Nasty's and Tay-Tay's bodies were glued together as he had her leg locked on his shoulders.

"Oh, shit, baby! God damn!" she yelled as she grabbed Nasty's face and started licking and kissing all over him. Her body started shaking.

Sweat dripped off Nasty's body while he pumped in and out.

"Ten, nine, eight, seven, six," he gritted his teeth to say.

The two started trading thrust for thrust.

"Five, four, three, two, one!"

"Oh, lord!" Tay-Tay yelled as she elevated her pelvis.

"Happy New Year's," Uno and Punkin said at the same time as they came in unison. Uno shut his eyes as he collapsed on top of Punkin.

"Ahhh, shit!" LR yelled as he tilted his head back and shot off down High-High's throat. He looked down at her, grinned, and then poured drinks everywhere.

"Happy New Year!" he yelled, running his fingers through her hair as she continued to suck his dick until the last drop was out.

Chapter 4

Bright and early that Monday morning, Uno was in their apartment's parking lot, sitting behind Punkin's old car tints. After returning from the trip, the two spent the rest of their time hugged up inside. Uno had earned major points in her book for showing her such a good time and putting his business aside for her.

"Be safe and call me the minute you get to the business. Go get our paper," she said, then kissed him on the lips.

***

By lunch time, Uno was walking through the salon, barber shop, and restaurant door, ready to start his week off. The parking lot was packed when he pulled into it. He guessed it was because everybody partied so hard over the weekend, and it was time to get back to work later that week.

Uno sat behind his cherrywood desk to look over the mail and the books. Over the past month, the business had cleared over $150,000 after everything was paid for. To show love for their hard work, Uno hit all the employees with a five-hundred-dollar bonus. Everyone deserved every dollar because they had busted their asses, making all three businesses an overnight success.

Next, he had to check all their supplies to make sure everything was stocked. Then he went out to mingle with the customers and employees. From the outside, looking in, one would think Uno was older than his age from the way he carried himself.

Uno called Kerry into his office after he had made all his rounds and brought her up to speed on his plans for the business for that year. Kerry didn't say a word as she jotted down notes so she could let the staff know.

Uno kept extra clothing in his office, so he changed into some street gear before hopping into the car and cruising around the city. Before going on his trip, he had done his homework, so he knew every part of the city where he wanted to set up a spot. He cruised the streets, stopping at all of Beeper's, Red's, and Man-Man's spots to see the action. While driving, he took in the city. He loved Indianapolis, but he didn't see himself there anymore after spending his whole life there. Plus, they were making money. He had to make sure he, his crew, and his family were secure; with his plans for the streets, he had to make sure everyone was okay. He didn't take the time to calculate all the crew's money, but he knew they were sitting on over $1 million between all of them.

Uno was trying to figure out how Beeper, Red, and Man-Man ran their spots. At the moment, all three controlled more than 85 percent of the city. They had the city in a headlock. Uno was happy with the little 15 percent he and his crew were controlling, but he promised himself that he was going to turn the heat up in the streets until he was on top of the city.

He needed to add more soldiers to his crew because Beeper and Red's crew were at least forty or fifty apiece. Man-Man was that major also. He was under Red at one point, but now he was at least equal to him. In contrast, aside from himself, Uno's crew was only six deep, and that wasn't enough to go against the other crews. They needed to form a tight circle, and it was finally the day that he would put everything in motion.

Before he left for the trip, he watched a group of youngsters who had weed spots out post. Baby J turned him on to the little niggas. The crew was about ten deep, ranging from fifteen to twenty, but what stuck out the most to Uno was how they were going about handling their business.

Uno slowly cruised into the apartment and nodded his head at how they were moving. They had lookouts at the entrance and throughout the apartments, and they ran a tight ship, so every last person was able to get some money. He pulled in, parked, and rolled down his windows.

"What's good with ya, bro?" Tezzy, the leader of the crew, asked. Tezzy was more of a shooter, but he still had his grind on with the pounds.

"What's up? Let me get a QP of that Kush."

Tezzy gave one of the dudes a nod, and the dude rushed inside one of the apartments to grab the smoke.

"Yo, Tezzy, hop in and chop it up with me for a minute so I can put a bug in your ear," Uno said, popping the locks.

Tezzy walked over and hopped into the passenger side. "What it do?" he asked, sitting down.

"I'm not trying to be all up in your shit, but I'm trying to figure out how y'all business is doing," Uno said.

Tezzy was a little caught off guard by what he was asking. "I'm good," Tezzy said, looking at Uno like he was crazy.

When the little dude returned to the car with the QP, Uno handed him twelve hundred dollars in exchange for the smoke. He then grabbed a swisher from the box, busted it down the middle, dumped the tobacco, and started licking the blunt.

"But like I was saying,"—Uno stopped to lick the blunt again—"you ever thought about fucking with the work?"

"Naw, all I ever did was move weed and bust this pistol," Tezzy replied, tapping his waist.

"Y'all got a money location," Uno complimented as he puffed on the blunt and exhaled the cloud of smoke. "But

I'm talking 'bout making tens of thousands of dollars," he continued, passing the blunt to Tezzy.

The tens of thousands had Tezzy's mind jumping. He puffed on the blunt, in deep thought. He blew the smoke out as he pondered making more money.

"All you have to do is run it how you running your apartments now. The dope will sell itself. You can kick your feet up and watch the money roll in. I'm trying to build a team," Uno added to make the offer sweeter.

Tezzy just nodded his head. "I'm down with the team!" he said.

Uno smiled at the thought of Tezzy and his crew on their team as he continued to cruise through the city.

After securing a few dudes by Crew Life, Mad Dogg, Brightwood, and 10th Street, he had tripled the clientele he already had. He had a silly mouthpiece on him. He made everyone feel they were making the right move by fucking with him and his team. He'd made up his mind already that the only people he was going to let sit at his table were him, LR, Nasty, Lil' E, Mo-Mo, Tezzy, and Babyface, and he had to pick Fat D's mind to see.

By 6 p.m., Uno was down to his last stop. He stopped in front of Kim's in his hood on 25th Street. Just like clockwork, the four hustlers he was looking for were posted up in front of the store like a light pole. That crew, Nasty handpicked himself. They would be a big part of the team.

"What's popping over this way?" Uno asked after rolling down his window.

"What up, bro?" the crew greeted, walking up to the car and giving out love.

The crew respected Uno and his team, whereas others stood off to the side, hating on them. Crews across the city wished they were part of their team. The whole crew came home and turned up the heat.

"Y'all hop in for a minute. I want y'all to fuck with me while we burn some of this good shit," Uno said. After the crew hopped in, Uno looked at all of them. "I ain't fucking with y'all money by having y'all ride with me, am I?" Uno asked them.

"Shit, naw, but know if it was rocking, I wouldn't have hopped in unless my sack was gone," the one name Reese said.

"Good. Y'all niggas roll us some blunts," Uno said, handing them some blunts and smoke. While they cruised, Uno took the time to gather his thoughts before chopping it up with the young niggas. He hopped on the highway, then looked at the three in the back seat in his rearview mirror.

"I been watching y'all for some time now, so I know y'all be grinding out there, but I'm yet to see any one of y'all hopping in any car, so how is it that y'all gettin' money, but it's not one car between the four of y'all?" Uno asked.

"Really, we not worried about no car right now until our money get right, feel me? When we can, we will put our shit together and grab something small. Until then, we stacking," Reese said.

Uno nodded his head and understood that Reese was the leader, but he knew what he had to do to get them to join his team.

***

Uno took Reese, King, Ali, and Drake to the auction to grab some whips. Reese copped a Jaguar, King copped a Mustang GT, and Ali and Drake copped Camaro SSs.

Uno had a connect at the auction, the same person who got the BMWs and bikes for his family. Uno gave her half in money and the rest in dope. After paying for everything, all four hopped in their cars and followed Uno to Hometown Express Customs to pick out rims. Afterward, he took them next door to Hometown Express paint shop, where they picked out their colors and left their whips.

As Uno cruised back to the hood, he heard the crew talking amongst one another. Right then, their love for Uno and WSF grew. Uno looked in the rearview mirror at the three and saw the looks he knew too much about. They were hungry, and he planned to feed them until their stomachs blew.

"Let me know something. Are y'all tired of standing up in front of Kim's grinding? Because I know she is," Uno said.

"Fuck yeah, bro!" the crew yelled together.

Uno nodded his head in understanding as he smiled to himself.

"Check dig. That shit I just did came from me and my team. We did that because we respect the game. You see, I been out here by myself and grinding hard. I didn't want people to think I got what I got because of my brothers, so I invest in myself, so the question is, are y'all ready to do the same? I just dropped over $100,000 on y'all today. All I ask is y'all join my team and remain loyal to the family."

"Hell yeah! That's the start we need, bro!" Reese said, speaking up for the crew.

"I'm going to let y'all move weight," Uno said

"But you know Beeper and Red already have a few spots over our way that's doing numbers," Drake said.

"Nigga, fuck them niggas!" the crew said, looking at him crazy.

"Red don't be in the hood like that, but Beeper can get touched," Reese said, meaning every word.

Uno smiled as he cruised through the hood. "I like y'all little niggas' swag. I think I'm gonna give y'all crew the name BTG for *Born to Go*," Uno said. The crew ginned because they approved the new name.

"That crib right there would've been the perfect spot to set up shop and take over Beeper's shit," Reese said, pointing to a white house on the corner where they could see down two streets at once.

Uno pulled in front of the house and parked. Then he pulled out a set of keys and dropped them in Reese's hand. As soon as the keys hit Reese's hand, his mouth fell in his lap.

"Yeah, I grabbed that spot a few weeks ago after I did my homework on y'all and Beeper," Uno said, smiling. "But about Beeper, y'all got to handle that so y'all can take over his shit too."

In less than a week, BTG had gotten Beeper out of the way while he was sitting at a stoplight on 29th. They even cleaned up the house, adding motion lights and a privacy fence that ran around the whole house. The trap was up and running, so Uno fronted each one a brick, taking them to the next level.

Tezzy and his crew also had their spot booming with smoke and crack, but what really stood out to Tezzy was how the money was coming, and he didn't have to do shit.

Uno planned to make sure everyone under him copped bigger every time they came to get on that with him, and his team could sit back.

Chapter 5

Business had picked up over the previous few days, and things were falling into place. Uno was standing in the shower, letting the steamy water hit his body, preparing himself for the weekend. The night before, he had split the last of the work between everyone, and he knew that with the way business was booming, they would need to get right, asap. He put in another order with Jimmy. Life was looking up for them.

Twenty minutes later, Uno was on the highway. He had a couple of stops to make to pick up money from a few dudes he had fronted work. As Uno headed across the city, he called LR and Nasty and told them to meet him at Lil' E's in thirty minutes. Uno's phone wouldn't stop ringing. Business had doubled for him since adding the new crews. After hollering at all the crews, Misty popped into his mind.

Meanwhile in Texas, Misty was strutting through the restaurant in her thousand-dollar Proenza Schouler sandals, showing the workers exactly where she wanted to set the tables, grills, and chairs. The men smiled as they walked behind her, listening. Her Prada Candy fragrance was intoxicating, and the Ralph Lauren dress she was wearing had seduced the owner of the company into giving her half off. A lot still needed to be done in the restaurant. Being that it was on MLK street, it was accessible. Since the restaurant sat in a plaza, parking wouldn't be any trouble.

Hearing her phone, Misty excused herself for a minute. "Hey, boo!" Misty answered, smiling.

"How's things going up ya way?" he asked.

"Everything is on schedule," she replied, strutting through the restaurant.

"I'ma have the rest of that dust for you soon," Uno told her.

"Just keep me posted like a light pole," Uno said.

"Okay. Boo, you should see the place," she said in a happy tone.

"Send me some pictures, but check it out. I got to get off this phone so I can bust my moves, but I'll hit you later sometime," Uno said, then hung up.

***

Over at Beeper's old trap, his crew, Man-Man, and Two-Tall were sitting in total silence, looking crazy as hell. A crackhead hadn't come to their door in hours. Ever since Beeper had been killed, business had stopped for them. BTG's name was on everyone's tongues, so obviously, that was where all their clientele was going to get on from.

Rome walked through the front door with some blunts.

"Man, y'all should see the flow at those niggas BTG niggas' spot!" Rome said.

Everybody in the house looked at him like he was crazy.

The leader of Beeper's crew shook his head. Since Beeper had been gone, they'd been copping from Beeper and Man-Man's other cousin, Black.

"Black's gonna have to come down on this silly ass price if he wants us to help him move this work," Juice said. "This is a business. He gotta at least make a nigga be able to compete!"

The crew nodded their heads. Juice called Black to inform him of what the deal was.

"Y'all ready for me already?" Black asked when he picked up the phone.

Juice stepped out onto the porch. "Not yet. Shit ain't actually moving like that over this way," he said, holding his breath.

"What you mean, *ain't moving like that!*" Black yelled with an attitude as he hopped up out bed, pushing the female off his dick.

"Listen, Black. I'ma give it to you uncut, raw. Those niggas Uno and WSF is fucking up the whole city. A lot of the clientele we had are jumping ship and fucking with them niggas now. It's taking us almost a week now to move what we used to move in days. And a lot of people is complaining to me about those high ass prices," Juice lied.

"Let them niggas know it's not a game, so it is what it is! If Beeper was around, y'all would be moving that shit! You and Man-Man soft asses need to work that shit out over there!" Black said, then hung up, contemplating his next move.

Uno and WSF were stepping in the wrong lane if they thought they were going to be fucking with his paper.

***

Lil' E's living room and kitchen looked like a bank. Uno, Nasty, and Lil' E sat in the living room, and LR sat at the kitchen table, counting stacks of money.

"Now this is the type of shit I'm talking about!" Nasty said as he sat back with his feet on the table.

"Nigga, get your damn feet down," Uno said, knocking his feet off the table, then smiled. "I'm proud of y'all niggas for doing good!"

With a plug, they were smashing the streets. It had been a few weeks since Uno copped any work from Hip-Hop, and he was blowing up his and LR's phones every day.

Nasty pointed to the duffle bag sitting off to the side, smoking a blunt. "That's $250,000 right there."

"Yeah this is $125.000," LR said, setting the last stack of money on the floor.

Uno nodded his head as he counted the money he got from Reese and Tezzy. "I'm putting $400,000 with that $250,000 and $125,000."

"We still got money in the streets, too," Lil' E said, walking back into the room.

Nasty smiled while transferring all of the money from the table to the duffle bag. "Damn, bros. Sometimes, this shit don't feel real," Nasty said.

"Nigga, ya better believe this shit, and we just getting started!" Uno replied. "Just remember," Uno said, setting his blunt down. "It's easy for all of us to get this money, but it's hard to keep it. The game is so saturated with ignorance it's like a full-time job, staying out of jail, and a blessing at the same time to be breathing. The best thing we can do with our money is make our money work for us. You see, I opened up something for Punkin. That way, if the game somehow showed up at our doorstep, her and my seed would still be good." Uno looked at each one with each word he spoke.

Chapter 6

After a few days of grinding, Nasty found himself chilling in his living room, sipping Remy Martin and counting up his earnings. Life was getting good, and he lived for the weekends.

"What the fuck!" Nasty said after he was done counting the stack of money.

He sat back on the sofa, shut his eyes, and thanked God for all the blessings he'd sent his way. Nasty wasn't into church but believed in God. His head started sweating as he sat back up and looked down at the $400,000 that sat on his floor. He had never had so much money in his life.

Nasty sipped his drink, trying to figure out his next move. He had always dreamed of being rich, like every other kid in the world, and now it was at the tip of his fingers. After a few more flips, he would be good. He had plans to open a nightclub in the city, but he wanted it to be different than everyone's in the city. While loading stacks of money from the floor into a duffle bag, he thought about the upcoming expo the following week, and he knew everybody who was someone was going to be downtown to show off.

After loading $320,00 into the duffle bag and zipping it up, he took $20,000 from his safe and left $60,000 out.

***

Uno didn't know exactly when, but somewhere between flips, his stash had hit a little past the $1-million mark. He relaxed in the living room of his new baby mansion he'd moved into a few days earlier. It was a new year, so he had to switch things up to start it off right by upgrading his and Punkin's living arrangement.

He walked onto his balcony and took in the breathtaking view of the lake. He was deep in the game and was about to turn the city up, so he wanted to be able to relax in peace. He had to make sure his crew did the same. His mansion gave him a serene feeling. Feeling safe hiding inside the walls of his mansion, he looked around his living room with high ceilings and state-of-the-art home entertainment system. Cameras were placed throughout his house, and he had them on the pole light at the beginning of the block. He had the baddest kitchen he'd ever seen that he couldn't wait to cook in. He hit a button, and a secret wall came out of the floor, showcasing a two-hundred-inch screen. He depressed another button, and the screen came to life, right along with all the cameras.

While watching CNN, he called Nasty and LR to see what was up with them.

"What's good, playa? LR answered.

"Hold on," Uno said, clicking Nasty in.

"What it do?" Nasty picked up.

"What you niggas got going on?" Uno asked.

"Shit. On my way out ya way?" Nasty said.

"Me, too, LR!" yelled.

"Damn, nigga, what you so damn hype for?" Uno asked LR.

LR laughed. "Nigga, I'ma show y'all why I'm so hyped up. I'll be there in about an hour."

"Alright, bro. I'll be waiting on ya," Uno said, hanging up with LR.

"Nigga, I'm about to pull up in a minute," Nasty said.

"Coo, nigga." Uno hung up.

Ten minutes later, Nasty pulled up to the security gate at Uno's mansion. "Buzz me in, nigga!" he said when Uno answered.

Uno watched the cameras, waiting for Nasty to turn the corner. *'What the fuck is he doing?'* he wondered when the only car he saw turning the corner was a Lamborghini. "I know this nigga didn't," he said to himself as he headed to the front door.

Sure enough, Nasty was sitting behind the driver's seat of the Lamborghini.

"Well, I'll be damned," Uno said, smiling while walking around the car.

"What it do?" he asked a smiling Uno.

Uno just stood there, smiling.

"This bitch is hard. Check out the inside," Nasty told him, opening the door to showcase its interior. "Jump in, bro?" Nasty said

Uno hopped in and started listening to Nasty talk about every feature.

"And I just had Hometown Express Customs rush order me some shoes for it!" Nasty bragged. "It set a nigga back just a little. I gave your car connect all of the money, and she gonna work it out to where it looks like I was making payments."

Uno's phone buzzed that someone was at the gate. "Who this?" He pressed a button on his phone, and the intercom came on.

"Nigga, open this gate," LR said.

"That was LR. He 'bout to pull up," Uno said.

A few minutes later, an all-black Porsche pulled around the corner. LR pulled next to Nasty's car and hopped out, smiling.

"I went and did the same thing," Nasty said, laughing.

Both of them turned toward Uno and at the same time said, "We know ya thinking we tripping." They dapped each other.

"I already made my mind up when I touched over $300,000, I was goin' to grab something," LR said.

"Here." Nasty threw him a bag.

He unzipped the bag and nodded.

"I got one, too," LR said.

Uno did the same thing with his bag. He zipped it back up, reached out, and put his arms around both of their shoulders.

"I'm really proud of y'all, bros," he said. "Earlier, I went and took Jimmy $500,000, and I'm going to take him another with this bread. Jimmy damn near choked when I told him I had $1 million for him."

Chapter 7

The carwash on 16th and MLK was jam-packed with every hustler in the city trying to get their toys washed for the expo.

It was Friday, the start of the expo. Every year afterward, they shut things down for the night, bumper-to-bumper. Traffic cruised up and down 38th Street, getting their shine on.

By 2 p.m., the expo was in full stride. Uno, Nasty, LR, Lil' E, and Babyface had just arrived and were strolling up the street, giving everybody love like they owned the city. Everybody was watching them, and they knew it.

"What's up, WSF!" was all the women were waving and saying to them as they continued their stroll.

Nasty and LR loved the attention. They both strolled with their chests poked out, heads high. After strolling around for about twenty minutes, they found their entire crew posted. Everybody was fresh from head to toe and draped in jewelry. The crew greeted the men like they were God's as they walked up because they were the reason for everyone's newfound success.

BTG wasn't there, because they all said they would pull up later on, but they were on grind mode. They knew everyone wanted to be at the expo, so they knew the stings needed someone to serve them.

Everybody arrogantly stood on the corner like they owned it. Females walked by, by the dozen, and praised them like they were kings. Punkin swaggered over with her girls and kissed Uno on the lips.

"Don't get fucked up out here," she told Uno before walking off.

Police stood off with disgrace on their face. The police officers weren't the only ones staring at them. Juice, his crew, and Man-Man stood across the street with envy in their eyes as they eyed Uno and his crew. Man-Man and Uno locked eyes. Neither one said or did anything, but the smile Uno gave Man-Man said all that needed to be said.

***

By 10 p.m., 38th Street was in full swing. Wet-painted whips with rims and loud sound systems strolled up and down 38th Street. Even the women were riding good. Everyone either parked in the BP parking lot on Fall Creek or the White Castle on 38th and Keystone. Weed smoke filled the air, and cups of liquor were being passed around. Females were cliqued up with their new outfits, walking the parking lot, trying to be noticed. Niggas cliqued up, repping different hoods, walking around, and making sure to stay by each other so if anything popped off, it would be easy to handle the problem.

Uno and his crew were parked across the street from White Castle, in Popeye's Chicken's parking lot, doing their own thing, at least forty deep. They were acting a fool, too.

Baby J came with his nigga TrapGod Rell from Mario; Scrill had shot down from South Bend with is clique; Tezzy pulled down with a few of his people; and JG shot down from Muncie.

Reese was on the set with his brand-new Yamaha YZF-R3 bike, trying to talk to every chick that strolled by.

The rest of BTG pulled into the parking lot and shut it down. They hopped out of their toys one by one. They showed off their mouths full of gold. All their toys had brand-new interiors, rims, paint, and loud sound systems.

Punkin posted, doing her thing with her friends. She even had Uno's little sister riding with her. Juice stood across the street in the White Castle parking lot, looking at BTG, having second thoughts about pulling up on them about short-stopping their stings. He knew he, his crew, and Man-Man were outnumbered.

Uno leaned on the hood of Punkin's BMW, smiling at what he had created. He had built a solid team in the city, and with the connections he'd made while locked up, he then had an out-of-town team, too. It was really time to take over shit in the streets. It was get down or lie down.

Uno answered his phone when it rang. "Hello?" He couldn't hear whoever was talking, because they were talking a mile a minute, so he stepped away so he could hear more clearly.

"Listen. Calm down and run that past me again," he said.

The caller explained everything to him more slowly and then ended by saying, "Oh, lord, Uno! I'm so scared right now!"

"I'm on my way," Uno said, then hung up. "We have to go, lil' sis," Uno said, hopping in her whip with her. "Something bad just happened, so get to the hood."

Twenty minutes later, Uno arrived in the hood. Big Dawg's girlfriend was nervously waiting for him while crying. She rushed into his arms when she spotted him. "Oh, Uno, I'm so happy you made it, but they shot your brother. The rest of the family just headed to the hospital."

"What happened?" their sister asked, crying.

Big Dawg's girlfriend hopped in the car, and they made it to the hospital in five minutes. Ant and the rest of the family stood inside the emergency room. For the next few hours, the family waited in the waiting area for a report on Big Dawg's condition. That night changed Uno's life and his family forever, when the doctor let them know Big Dawg didn't make it.

Chapter 8

Over the next week, Uno had been grinding non-stop to keep his mind off the fact someone killed his brother. He was lying across the bed, tired as hell. He fell into bed, fully dressed.

He'd spent all night cooking and splitting up all their dope. Punkin sent their daughter to her mother's house so she could help and spend time with Uno. She knew he was hurting badly because he looked up to his big brothers. Since the night of the expo, all Uno did was grind hard. He started showing Punkin how to cook and bag up the dope.

Uno hopped up, jumped in the shower, and let the hot water hit his head. Ten minutes later, he stepped out of the shower, grabbed a towel, and dried off. Uno was lost in his thoughts, thinking about all he had lost and gained. His thoughts were interrupted by the sound of his phone ringing. He quickly rushed into his bedroom to pick it up.

"Hello?"

"Hey, baby! I love you!" Punkin yelled in his ear.

Uno sat down on the bed and smiled. "Where you at, baby?" he asked.

"I had to bust a few moves. I will be home soon," she said, smiling on the other end of the phone.

"Alright, sexy," he said, then hung up.

After hanging up, he grabbed a new pair of Lacrosse boxer briefs and threw them on. He then sprayed on a few squirts of Jordan Blue, then got dressed.

As Uno headed into the city, Ant called to check on him to make sure he was okay.

The two talked for a hot second until their mother's phone number popped up. Uno promised Ant he would be safe and okay, then he clicked over to talk to their mother. He and his mother joked and laughed on the phone until he pulled up in the dealership parking lot.

Uno hopped out with his Lacrosse duffle bag. An hour later, Uno stepped out of the dealership with keys to a brand-new Aston Martin. Hometown Express Customs was just pulling into the parking lot when he stepped outside. He threw on his four-hundred-dollar Saint Laurent shades, tossed Hometown Express Customs the keys to his new toy, and then headed to have fun with his people.

When Uno pulled up on the 610 block of Eugene, it was fat. The air smelled like weed from all the blunts being passed around. The crew showed Uno love when he stepped out of his car.

Mo-Mo, Lil' E, Nasty, LR, Reese, the rest of BTG, Punkin, Tay-Tay, and Rabbitt were out chilling, having fun with each other. For the next few hours, they had fun, getting their drink, smoke, and eat on. The whole hood came out to the get-together. So many people were coming down the block that it was bumper-to-bumper at one point.

"I got to get up out of here," Uno said, giving the niggas dap and the kids hugs. "I'll see you at home in an hour or two, so be there."

Around 6 p.m., Uno pulled in front of their house as Punkin was walking out of the house, looking stunning in her green Versace dress, confidently strolling out to the car with her Roger Vivier purse. Uno smiled as he inhaled her fragrance when she sat in the car, and her hair was laid.

"Hey, baby!" Punkin said as she leaned over and kissed him.

"What you up to?" he asked.

"Nothing, baby." She blushed. "Here's the address," she said, typing it into the GPS.

Twenty minutes later, Uno pulled into the parking lot of a five-star restaurant, and the two were quickly led to a secluded table in the corner. Uno stared at Punkin with suspicion as the waitress lit the candles on the table. A bottle of Assyrtiko, chilled Champagne rested on the table.

Uno looked around at the well-designed restaurant. The lighting seemed just right.

"When we gonna eat?" Uno asked.

Punkin smiled. "I already handled that."

Before Uno could say anything, the server walked out with a beautiful platter with tender steaks, mushrooms, onions, and sauce. A platter of garlic shrimp linguine followed a bowl of potatoes, accompanied by a tossed green salad.

Uno was high, so he grabbed a plate and immediately dug in. While Uno ate, Punkin started blushing after she put a gift on the table. He smiled at her before opening it then sat with his mouth open when he saw what was inside.

Uno was so happy because he planned to do it for himself, too.

"Thank you, baby! When you get this made?" he asked, holding the 'R.I.P. Big Dawg' chain in his hand. Uno smiled. It was amazing how Punkin always thought about him.

An hour later, Uno was dropping Punkin off at her mother's house.

***

Nasty and LR couldn't have picked a better place to chill for the night. Uno told them they had to start surrounding themselves with people with money. They couldn't be hood all their lives, even though, sometimes, one would have to go back to their roots.

There were men and women who looked like lawyers, doctors, or just had money seated in booths, decked out, telling jokes, having fun, puffing on cigars, and sipping their drinks.

Uno felt like a million bucks as he strolled through the club, looking for Nasty and LR in his Balmain sweater and Italian slacks. Thanks to some amphibian, he was sporting a Balmain alligator belt to complement the matching gators on his feet. Uno made his way to the booth.

Every eye in the building was on him as he sat down in the booth with the two. The club was swarming with beautiful women who kept pulling up on them, asking if they played sports. Uno just laughed, while Nasty and LR told them yes.

"We ballers," LR told one female.

"I see y'all funds are jumping off," a woman who had just sat in their booth said.

"Do we know you?" Uno asked.

"My name is Nicole Sebree," she said to them, showing off her sparkling smile.

Nasty noticed she was by herself.

Nicole was a fine sister. Her almond complexion, big eyes, and sexy, puffy cheeks would catch any man's attention. Her lips were so sexy that Uno almost leaned in and kissed her. Her form-fitting Milly Jacquard minidress hugged her. Her skin had a glow, and her fresh French pedicure and manicure showed that she was on her grown woman.

As Uno's eyes made their way back up her body, he could tell she worked out from her well-toned legs and arms.

Nicole saw all three of them checking her out, so she smiled. "Are y'all done?" she asked as she sipped her drink. "So, Uno, LR, and Nasty—" she began.

"Hold up," LR interrupted with a raised brow. "We never told you our names."

Nicole raised a brow. "Come on now. WSF. Who in the city don't know y'all? The streets talk. Plus, my cousin let me know who y'all was when we saw y'all at the expo."

"So why you didn't pull up on us and say anything then?" Uno asked.

"One, because y'all had too many groupies around y'all, and I would never be in that type of group, and two, because I'm about that bag, so this is all business," Nicole said.

"First, who is your cousin?" Uno asked.

"JG."

"Okay, talk to us," Uno said, gesturing with his hand.

"Cool. Look at y'all selves. For example, from y'all clothes, jewelry, and cars outside, y'all have over $2 million invested."

This bad muthafucka on top of her game,' Uno thought as Nicole continued totaling up what they were wearing.

"Damn, you must be into fashion?" Uno laughed.

"Got jokes," Nicole said. "But look at it from the outside, in, and tell me what y'all see."

"I got this, bro," LR said, setting his drink down and looking Nicole in the eyes. "I see three niggas from the westside of town that get it out of the mud and now balling," he replied arrogantly.

Nicole shook her head and twisted her face. "I'ma tell you what I saw when I looked at y'all. I saw a nice business or crib in a nice part of the city."

"Real estate?" Uno asked.

"Yeah. That's where the money is right now. Y'all brothers out here in the streets need to stop and think about how the white man is always a step ahead. You see, a brother would go out to a strip club, throw a $100,000, or buy some jewelry—but would say no on investing in prosperow or a business," Nicole preached.

"We already—" Uno cut LR off.

"Let her finish, so sit back, lil' bro," Uno said, sitting back and taking in every word Nicole's lips spat out, even though his brothers had already gamed him. Plus, she didn't know he'd already invested his money, but he let her continue to see what type of game she would lay out.

"See, with real estate, you buy foreclosures. It could cost one dollar up. Going after foreclosures, you already have equity in the property when you close the deal. That way, you won't lose."

"So, what you get out of all this?" Uno asked.

"Okay, I get a percent and get to put some brothers up on the white man's game. I know y'all out here grinding hard, so with the game I'm leaving y'all, y'all would be about to make sure your families are good if the Feds pull up at y'all doorstep. Most brothers don't think about the future."

"How we know you not the Feds?" Uno asked, looking her in the eyes.

She laughed at him while waving her hand. "Nigga, ask about me. I'm born and raised right here in this city, and I'm from 4-Block. My brother Budds, but you may know him as Sam. He fucks with Murder, with the VVS in his mouth. Well, Budds sent me out of town to go to school a few years back to get my master's degree in business. Now I'm working for Ruthie Real Estate Company. I just moved back six months ago because I saw the market was wide open, so I jumped on it."

"What does that have to do with you bein' the police?" Uno asked with a serious face. "And I do know your brother and Murder. They some solid niggas."

"Anyway, boy, boo. I'm a hydro head, got stolen cable, and these heels I have on came from my booster that I have on speed dial."

"Okay. Say we believe you. Then what?" Nasty spoke for the first time.

"We going to clean that $50,000 you have on your arm," she said, looking at Nasty.

"I'm curious. Why you choose us?" Uno asked.

"Really, after I observed y'all a few times, I knew y'all crew was different. Then, when my people let me know y'all was risk takers, I knew y'all was nothing like these clowns out here. If y'all allow me to show y'all a few new tricks with money…" she commented, sipping on her drink.

"How much you think we need?" Uno asked, really feeling what she was been talking about.

"Whatever y'all willing to put down, but probably somewhere around $100,000."

"What about we all put $100,000 apiece?" Nasty asked.

Nicole spat her drink on the floor. "Damn, $300,000? I see y'all with the money team for real. How about y'all come by my office Monday morning? That way, I can show y'all a few businesses and properties that are up for sale."

"Sounds good to us." Uno nodded.

Chapter 9

That Monday, Uno, LR, and Nasty walked into Nicole's office, smelling and looking good. When they walked in, they sat down, and she got right down to business. She set her briefcase on the table, pulling out a list of properties and businesses.

"This is the list of foreclosures around this way. I call them top doggs properties because they're usually located in prime areas that are family-friendly."

"How long we talking about?" Uno asked.

"These properties are usually in good condition. It really all depends on the caliber of people you hire to repair them. I will say maybe three or four months, tops, and that includes closing and everything," she said.

"I'm trying to open a club, so I need to see some shit I can build, feel me?" Nasty spoke.

Nicole showed them the list of properties under $125,000 and then hit a few keys on her laptop. She spun the screen around so they could see all the properties and businesses listed under the $225,000 range.

"Are y'all ready to go look at some places?" she asked.

"We been ready," LR said, walking out of the office.

For the next few hours, the four of them visited different properties that Nicole had on her list. They followed Nicole as she walked through each place and told them the ins and outs. Seeing Nicole in action turned Uno on. She knew her homework, and that impressed Uno.

By the end of the day, the four were seated at a table at Applebee's, trying to reach a decision. They had narrowed their selections down to four places that were in the range of $100,000 to $200,000. Those needed less work done.

Uno, LR, and Nasty looked over the paperwork. The total for all four places came to $525,000.

"So, what y'all think so far?" she asked.

Everyone just smiled.

"Let's get it rolling!" Uno said.

Nicole gave them a warm smile. "Y'all won't be disappointed. I'll type up the paperwork, contact the owners, and then negotiate the best deal we can get."

"It's a wrap," LR said.

"Check this out. You telling me that you can purchase any properties in the city that's on the market?" Uno asked with an idea popping into his mind.

"Yeah, all I need is the address. I'll run it through the system, see who owns them, and see if they're willing to sell," she replied.

Uno grinned. "I'll get the addresses to you first thing tomorrow," he said, then stood and shook Nicole's hand before they left.

Chapter 10

The week had blown by fast. Misty had hung up her stripper heels to devote her time to getting the restaurant up and running. She was happy it was Wednesday, and she would be hooking up with Uno and his people to hang out with them and to pick up the rest of the money he had for her.

She stood in her walk-in closet, looking at all of her clothes. She thumbed through her wardrobe, searching for the right outfit to catch Uno's eye.

"Girl, wear that dress you grabbed the other day," Kandi said, followed by London.

"And his brothers better be fine, too," London commented.

Misty laughed but grabbed the form-fitting Armani dress with a pair of matching boots. She undressed in front of the girls and rushed to the bathroom to take her bath.

Twenty minutes later, Misty was dressed, standing in front of the mirror, letting London put on her makeup. She licked her luscious lips and inspected herself. They went into the living room, where Misty checked her paperwork to make sure it was in order.

She had taken pictures so she could show Uno how hard she'd been working. She wanted him to see before and after. She even had all the receipts to account for everything she spent.

***

LR had his Porsche on cruise control as he, Nasty, and Uno drove down the highway. The highway patrol had been side by side with him for the last ten minutes, but off and on, they'd been following him for the past few miles. Altogether, they had over two hundred grand in the car, so they remained calm and kept their composure like the G's they were.

Life was good for them. Nicole had sent all three texts and informed them that the deal was going through on all four places. They could add property investors to their growing resume. They all respected Nicole. She was about her business and saved them money in the process. She would be a valuable asset to their organization, and they each planned to give her a $5,000 bonus to show their appreciation when they touched back in the city.

By 2 p.m., LR was taking the Texas exit. Uno whipped out his cell and called Misty to see where she and her girls were.

"Hello?" She answered with a smile on the other end of the phone.

"Where ya at?" he asked.

"I'm less than ten minutes away from the address I texted you," she answered, speeding down the street.

Uno, LR, and Nasty were chilling at the mall, admiring all the eye candy walking through the building. Uno looked up and saw Misty and her girls walking toward them. She was smiling, showing off her pretty teeth. Uno greeted Misty with a hug and a kiss.

"Mm, I missed you so much, baby," Misty said, hugging him tighter.

"I missed you a lot, too," he said, admiring her body.

"Excuse you? Hello, my name is London, and this is Kandi," she said to Uno, eyeing LR and Nasty.

"Yeah, I remember y'all. These are my two brothers, LR and Nasty," Uno said.

"Damn, Nasty? I like that name," Kandi said, sitting next to him with London moving toward LR.

Misty and Uno got down to business, while the other four did them. She opened her briefcase, handed Uno a handful of papers with all the financial statements, and then handed him her phone so he could see the progress the restaurant was making.

"You ain't playing, are you?" Uno asked as he looked over everything.

"Why would I be?" she asked with a smile on her face.

"That's why you're on my team," he replied, sliding a Louis Vuitton bag with a box inside over to her. "A little something."

Misty opened the box. "Oh my God! How you know I wanted this bag?" she asked, taking out the handbag.

"I ordered that for you," Uno said, smiling.

"You're a amazing man," she said, then leaned forward and kissed him.

After finishing their meal, they gathered their things and wandered through the mall, talking.

"So, tell me something. Do you see yourself ever setting down?" Misty asked him as she swung his hand.

Uno looked at her and smiled. "Someday, but not yet," he replied.

After exiting the mall, the two laughed and joked.

"So, I guess this is it for now?" Misty asked as they stood next to LR's car.

Uno grabbed her chin and pulled her into his arms.

The two rested their foreheads against each other's, and then Misty kissed him. She pulled away when her pussy lips got wet. "Damn!" she said, taking a deep breath.

"You did it," Uno said, smiling.

"Well, until next time," she said, a little choked up.

"I'll be back this way in a few weeks," Uno said, caringly kissing her forehead.

Misty smiled then waved goodbye as he, LR, and Nasty hopped in the car.

"Misty!" Uno yelled.

"Yeah?" she replied, spinning around, hoping he said he would spend the night with her.

"You're forgetting something, ain't you?" he asked as he held up the bag that contained the money she needed to wrap things up with the restaurant.

Misty had an attitude as she walked over to grab the bag.

Uno told LR to wait until she pulled off into traffic. "We about to pull up on Baby J. This where he been resting his head... Big cuz, what it do? I'm in your stomping grounds right now," Uno said to Baby J as soon as he picked up.

"Damn, cuz, I had to hit New York for a hot second," Baby J said.

"Well, love, and I will be back this way soon," Uno replied and hung up.

Chapter 11

It was the day men and women showed their significant others just how they cared for them. Flowers and balloons were being delivered all across the world.

Punkin was chilling in their kitchen, eating breakfast that Uno had ordered a professional chef to cook for her. She wished he didn't have to go out of town, but it was business, so she understood. Along with the chef, he had some roses and balloons delivered and told her to take herself on a shopping spree to buy whatever her eyes liked. She just wanted to be held by Uno.

***

Misty rushed to her front door when she heard her doorbell ring for the second time.

"Here I come!" she yelled.

A UPS deliveryman was standing on her front porch with a beautiful bouquet of roses, a bear, and a box of chocolates. Misty stood there, frozen. After a few seconds, she took the roses, bear, and candy. She thanked the man and shut her door. She smiled as she shook her head after reading the card. Uno was an amazing man.

***

Tay-Tay was sitting in the salon chair, getting the latest gossip on the streets, when a UPS man walked inside and asked for her. Hearing her name, she cautiously said something. The deliveryman motioned for her to give him a minute before he headed out to his truck.

Tay-Tay placed her hand over her mouth when the deliveryman returned and handed her a beautiful bouquet of roses.

"Umm. somebody's on their shit!" the stylist joked. All the women in the salon just laughed.

Tay-Tay just shook her head. "Nasty, you truly an amazing man," she whispered as she took the car out and read it.

***

Rabbitt was just about to walk out of her crib when a UPS man came to the front door and delivered a beautiful bouquet of roses with a bear and chocolates. She thanked the deliveryman as she sniffed the flowers. She took out the card and read it. A huge smile appeared on her face as she headed to the kitchen to put her flowers in water.

Needless to say, that day, Uno, LR, and Nasty made a statement. They proved that no matter where they were, they could still show love to those in their life.

Chapter 12

A few weeks later, Black received calls back-to-back from landlords telling him that they had sold the properties, and he had to talk with the new owners of the properties.

Black cruised the city, heated. Who the fuck were these new landlords? "Fuck!" Black cursed. He needed those spots in the location they were in because that was how he made his bread. It had taken him months to build those spots up.

After trying to contact the new landlords one last time, Black hung up when he got the voicemail again. He pulled up to one of his spots and saw a police car parked outside.

"What the fuck?" Black cursed.

The police stood by his car while Juice and his crew exited the trap. Black knew when word got out, he would be the talk of the town. That evening, Black and his crew stuck around to see who was going to pull up to the spot.

As Black sat across the street from the spot on 25th, his blood started to boil when he saw Uno's crew pull up, and the little niggas started moving stuff in. Steam came out of Black's ears, watching how Uno's crew immediately started booming. What put the knife in the cake was when Uno slowly drove past him in his Aston Martin, winked, laughed, and then honked his horn.

"You just started a war," Black said to himself.

***

In a week, Uno managed to take control of more of the city. For the past few months, the game had been showing him and his crew mad love. They deserved it, though. He'd been putting in silly hours, helping Punkin run her business, constantly talking to Misty about her business, and grinding from sunup to sundown to finance everything. Not only had he secured a connect, he was also self-made and built the empire from the ground up with the help of his team.

He thought about his crew and how far they had come. They were a family getting major paper, and they were highly respected in the city. Everyone's lives were taking a turn for the better, and they had gotten toys, cribs, clothes, jewelry, bad hoes, and plenty of money.

Instead of enjoying the day, Uno was the type who worried about the next day. He knew his team was up, but he also knew Black had something in the making.

Chapter 13

Man-Man and Two-Tall had been forced to join Juice and his crew.

Since Uno was supplying Reese with dope, they literally shut down Juice's entire operation. Black knew people in Richmond, so he broke a deal with Man-Man and Two-Tall. Black supplied all of the dope, and Man-Man, Two-Tall, and Juice's crew could set up shop over in Richmond. Man-Man and Two-Tall didn't agree with the arrangement and hated that they had to travel back and forth. They felt like bitches because Uno and his crew had literally muscled them out of the city, and they hadn't done anything in return.

"So, Black, I know we ain't finna sit around and let them WSF niggas just push us out of the city and steal all of our clientele like this. We done bitched up and just cut out of the city! You know we the butt of all the jokes around the city?" Juice ranted.

"Yeah!" the entire crew said.

Everybody was hot. Not only had Uno and WSF taken their clientele, but they were the crew to see in the city. All their bitches, girlfriends, or baby mamas were fucking someone on their team. Every time they turned around, all they heard was WSF.

Black quietly paced the room with his hands in front of him. WSF had connected their dots good, and now they had enough manpower to win a war, so he had to think of a power move. He knew what war was and meant.

"How many spots do they have that we know of?" Black asked.

"Shit, counting our spots, twelve around the city!" Juice said.

"Alright, here's the plan," Black said, rubbing his chin.

***

Man-Man, Two-Tall, Juice, and Rome were all dressed in black, sitting in a car across the street from Reese and his crew's spot on 25th Street.

"You sure this is where them niggas keep all their dope and money?" Juice asked as he cocked his Springfield SOCOM II.

"Hell yeah, I'm positive," Man-Man lied.

Two-Tall just shook his head. Man-Man had convinced Black that Reese was one of the major niggas in WSF's operation and that he was selling weight. Truth be told, Man-Man was shitty that Uno and LR pulled his coattail that day on the block. Also, he felt they were involved in the deaths of Flow and Beeper. He just didn't know.

"How much dope and bread do you think them niggas got in there?" Rome cocked his gun and asked.

"One of the little niggas mess with their female sister I be fuckin', and he be pillow talking, so she told us they keep at least $100,000 and a few bricks in there," Man-Man lied.

Juice looked in the back seat at Man-Man and Two-Tall.

"Y'all niggas ready?" Juice asked. "Let's handle this."

Reese and his crew were inside, counting up the profit from the day's grind. They made a little over $15,000 apiece. Reese grabbed the walkie-talkie off the table when he heard it chirp. "What's up, Drake?"

"It's four niggas with guns creeping along the side of the house next door," Drake whispered as he stared on from across the street.

"Heat!" Reese told his crew, and everyone rushed for their guns.

"One is on his way up to the front porch, and the other one's creeping on the side of the house," Drake whispered.

Inside the house, Reese hit all the lights. He and his crew were sitting in total darkness. Everyone was in position, waiting for their assailants to kick in the door so they could light their asses up with lead.

There was a knock at the door, so Reese peeped out the window and saw a shadow. Reese gave his crew a silent three-count, then busted the front window and started dumping rounds on the porch.

"Ahhh! Shit!" Rome cried as three bullets entered his shoulder.

"Oh, shit!" Juice yelled when he saw Rome's body spin around and hit the stairs in front of the house. Juice returned fire as he rushed and grabbed Rome off the stairs, dragging him around the house.

Man-Man and Two-Tall were in shock when they saw the rest of Reese's crew come from both sides of the house, busting their guns at them. Two-Tall returned fire.

Juice tossed Man-Man the keys. "Go get the car, nigga!" he yelled to Man-Man as he fired more while dragging Rome's bloody body behind the next-door neighbor's house.

Man-Man dashed through the gunfire like he was running for his life to grab the car. His heart pumped a hundred miles per hour as he heard sirens rapidly approaching. Seconds later, Man-Man pulled up in the alley, and Two-Tall ran over and assisted Juice with putting Rome in the back seat.

Reese ran out, took aim, and shot out the car window.

"Got damn!" Man-Man yelled, covering his head while glass shattered all over their bodies.

"Bitch, drive!" Juice yelled at Man-Man. Man-Man mashed the gas and sped off.

Reese smiled, then hopped in the car with his crew and sped off.

Juice was in the back seat, hysterical as he held Rome in his arms and watched him slip away. "You niggas set us up!" Juice fumed. "Who you niggas with?" Juice asked, putting his gun to the back of Man-Man's head.

"I promise, if my cousin dies, I'ma kill you, nigga!"

Man-Man made it to the emergency room in record-breaking time. Juice grabbed Rome out of the backseat, and then Man-Man sped off. Juice toted Rome into the emergency room.

"We need a fucking doctor!" Juice yelled.

That night, Black's entire plan went south. His crew had been unsuccessful. It seemed to him that Uno had a heads-up. Black sat at his kitchen table, contemplating his next move. There had been casualties on both ends. His crew had shot Holla-Holla at one of WSF's spots, and Rome was in critical condition.

These WSF niggas is really fucking with my bread!

Chapter 14

Uno was coming from making his rounds, checking on his crew, and making sure everyone was cool. It was evident that Black and his crew were responsible for last night's attempts at his spots. Harm had been done on both ends.

Rome was in critical condition, fighting for his life. The bullets that hit him had pierced his spine, paralyzing his body from the neck down.

Reese was inside the BTG, bragging about how he let his pistol talk for him that night. Police had swarmed the spot, so Uno, LR, and Nasty shut down and had Reese and BTG's crew double up with Mo-Mo and Lil' E at their spot and run shifts.

Uno, LR, and Nasty talked out everything and knew it was best for no one to retaliate yet or until one gave the word. War would cost them too much money, and they had a gut feeling that what Black was trying to do was get them off their square.

Black's little attempt didn't hurt the WSF or any of their crews, but in return, it hurt them more.

***

It had been a while since Big Dawg's funeral. All of Big Dawg's family was gathered around the oval table in the conference room, waiting to hear Big Dawg's last will and testament.

"Hi everyone, I'm Sarah Land, the executor of Chandler Drew's Last Will and Testament. We're waiting on one more person, and then we can start," she said, looking at her watch. Everyone looked around and started whispering amongst each other, wondering who the missing person was.

The day before, when Alexis received a certified envelope telling her that her presence was requested at the reading for her son's father's last will and testament, chills and bumps popped all over her body.

After the doors opened on the sixth floor, Alexis exited the elevator and headed to suite 600.

"A few more minutes, and we're gonna get started," Sarah said. Sarah looked up toward the door and smiled when their expected guest cracked open the door.

Alexis, Big Dawg's son's mother, stood at the door and smiled. Big Dawg's sister and mother rolled their eyes and tilted their noses up.

"Hello, are you Alexis Jenkins?" Sarah asked.

"Yes, I'm Alexis," she replied as the two shook hands.

Sarah grabbed Big Dawg's will out of her folder.

"I'm sure, by now, everyone knows why we're here today. This is the last will of Mr. Omar, aka Big Dawg," Sarah said as she proceeded. "This is a legal document, made in accordance with the state of law." After explaining the purpose of the will, Sarah got right down to business.

"To my son's mother, I leave my houses on 25th Edgemont and Udell. I also leave a sum of $200,000," Sarah said. "To my mother, I leave the land I have in Cuba, the sum of $200,000, and any three of my cars. To my brothers, Uno and Ant, and my little sister, Barber Jane, I leave the sum of $200,000 each, as well as my business, divided between the three. Also, Uno and Ant, I leave my timeshares in Costa Rica, my vehicles, and the land in Texas."

Alexis sat there the whole time in shock. All that kept running through her head was $200,000.

"This concludes the reading of the will," Sarah said, then stood and thanked everyone for coming.

"Uno and Ant, can I speak to both of you for a minute?" Sarah said.

"What's good?" Uno said, walking over.

Sarah smiled and handed both envelopes. "He wanted me to give y'all this, along with two keys to his safe. Y'all can go into my office and read it," she told them.

Both walked into Sarah's office, sat down at her desk, and pulled out the contents of the envelopes. They both had smiles on their faces as they flipped through pictures of them over the years. There was a letter in each envelope.

Dear brothers,

These letters say the same thing. If y'all reading this letter that means I'm dead and gone. I hope y'all can forgive me for not letting y'all know ahead of time but McDuffy from 2-6 killed me. We had some business and as y'all know he wanted to be the boss so he tried to cut me out by going to the other side. It's a key inside of the envelope. It's the key to my safe. There you both would find information on everyone on that list inside. Make sure y'all always keep that list safe because it's priceless and use it wisely.

Love Always,

Big Bro Dawg

Both brothers got teary-eyed after Uno read the letter. They looked inside the envelope and saw the paper with a key taped on it.

Later that night, Uno and Ant sat in a room in Uno's crib. Ant popped open Big Dawg's safe, and they both couldn't believe their eyes. Big Dawg had stocks, bonds, deeds to properties, and bank accounts totaling over $2 million, all in their names.

Big Dawg must have felt that he was going to get killed and made sure the two could take care of their whole family.

Uno couldn't do anything but look at the bank statement in his hand. He flipped through pictures of the Chief of

Police snorting cocaine with some young females, the mayor getting head from two black chicks, and he even had a few pictures of the DA doing all types of freaky things with girls and pets.

Chapter 15

Man-Man had gotten a big head when his plug Red went back to fronting him work. He was so blind by the pussy that bitch Ashley was putting on him. He got mad at Two-Tall for saying she was thick, so he'd been playing crazy ever since the connect came back around. Two-Tall was inquisitive about finding out if Ashley's pussy was to die for. The only thing keeping him from fucking over Man-Man was all the years of friendship, but if he was going to say fuck it, so was he. Two-Tall sat on his sofa and puffed on the blunt, while Juice talked on the phone. Between both, they only had $15,000. Black had been acting crazy, too.

"Let's go," Two-Tall said as both of them walked out of the house.

***

Jimmy sat up and looked Hip-Hop in the eyes so he could know he was speaking real words.

"Muthafucka, if I don't call you, you don't pop up at my place again unannounced. The only reason you're not dead is because I know your uncle!" Jimmy pointed his finger and yelled at Hip-Hop.

"My bad, but I thought you gave me your word," Hip-Hop said as McDuffy held him in a chokehold.

Jimmy just sat back in his chair, grabbed his drink, and took a sip. "I'm done with you, so don't call my line anymore," Jimmy said.

"So, after all the money I have dropped at your feet, this the thanks I get?" Hip-Hop asked.

Jimmy just waved his hand. "Uno and his team have brought me more money in the matter of two months than the entire time I've known you. You're finished! Make this the last time I see you because if I see your ugly ass again, you're gone!" Jimmy said, pointing at Hip-Hop.

"Bounce!" McDuffy forcefully pushed Hip-Hop off.

After walking Hip-Hop through the side door, McDuffy and Music surveyed the area to see if the coast was clear. Then they ushered Hip-Hop around toward the back of the building.

"Nigga, I'ma gonna call you," McDuffy said. Music blocked them. That way, no one from the front could see them.

"Why?" Hip-Hop asked.

"Let's just say we not feeling the way Jimmy is rocking right now, and we hate that nigga Uno ass. Now get up outta here! We'll call you soon. and this conversation never happened."

Confused, Hip-Hop just went and hopped in his car, hot that Uno found his plug and got him to cut him out of the picture.

***

Two-Tall and Juice had been following Man-Man all day. They learned what spots were jumping and what he did during the day. They just so happened to be driving in a 2-G when they saw Man-Man's new Lincoln truck sitting in Ashley's driveway. Two-Tall never knew the bitch stayed right in the hood. They sat in the cut behind 5 percent tints across the street, dressed in all black. They snorted a line apiece of powder. Two-Tall picked up the habit from being around Juice. Juice went from snorting lines to grams.

"Let me go in by myself," Juice said, hyped up.

"Okay, listen. Go in there and get everything they have, but don't kill nothing," Two-Tall said.

"Coo'," Juice said, hopping out and running across the street to the back door. He walked around the house, looked in one window, and saw the kids lying down. He continued to the next one, where he saw Man-Man and Ashley fucking. Returning to the back door, he knocked out the small window on the door, making little noise. The sounds of Trey Songz blasted from the bedroom as he tiptoed slowly down the hallway.

"Damn, this nigga in there making love to that bitch," Juice joked as he pulled his mask over his head and stood, listening.

He cracked the door open and slowly tiptoed inside the room. He stood and watched as Man-Man arched his back, fucking Ashley from the back. Juice's dick got hard, listening to Ashley moan and talk dirty. Juice stroked his dick as he bent down and saw Ashley creaming all over Man-Man's dick. Right when he saw Man-Man about to nut, he cocked his pistol.

Man-Man and Ashley, disentangled and terrified, scooted back to the headboard.

Juice looked at Ashley with a smirk behind the mask. She shook her head no, knowing what his eyes were saying. She then grabbed the sheet and covered her body. Juice stood there, still stroking his dick as he talked.

"Is this pussy good?" Juice grinned. Man-Man protectively grabbed Ashley and held her close to his chest.

"She ain't got shit to do with what you came here to do," Man-Man said, not knowing why he was there.

Juice looked around the room for the first time and saw a book bag leaning on the wall. He walked over to the bag to see what was inside. When he unzipped it, a smile appeared on his face as he looked at the two kilos and a few stacks of money.

Man-Man bit the inside of his mouth. That shit always happened to him while dealing with this bitch.

"You, get over in the corner!" Juice ordered Man-Man.

Man-Man got up and dropped to his knees while facing the corner.

Ashley nervously stood, waiting for her instructions.

"Bring that ass here, girl. Get back on all fours, and scoot yo' ass to the edge of the bed," Juice told her.

Ashley looked over at Man-Man, who was facing the wall, then did as she was told.

"You see, nigga. I'm going to show you how to fuck some pussy," Juice said, ramming his dick into Ashley's already wet pussy.

Ashley was in tears as Juice's big dick stretched her insides. All types of thoughts ran through Ashley's mind as Juice's dick started to feel good inside her pussy. Her pussy came three times back-to-back, and at that moment, Juice passed Man-Man on her list of dicks. None took Nasty's spot.

"Damn, I know why you and Nasty is crazy about his pussy!" Juice joked as he went in and out of her pussy. "Throw that pussy back, bitch!" he slapped her on the ass and said.

Ashley started to really get into the mix and worked her pussy muscle on his dick.

"Damn, bitch, you know how to fuck, don't you? Turn around and get this nut," Juice told Ashley as she spun around and started sucking the head of Juice's dick.

Juice pumped and pumped her mouth until he was about to nut, then pulled out and busted all in her mouth.

Ashley forgot Man-Man was in the room and that she was getting raped for a minute. Juice pulled up his pants, lifted his mask, and winked at Ashley as he grabbed the book bag and backed out of the room.

Two-Tall saw Juice running toward the car, so he got ready. Hopping in, Juice just smiled as he began to let Two-Tall in on what'd just happened.

"Bro, I'm telling you, that pussy is to kill for," Juice said, opening the bag for Two-Tall to see.

"What? You just raped Ashley?" Two-Tall asked, not liking the sound of that shit. Two-Tall pulled down Edgemont, where it was dark. "Go put that bag in the trunk," he told Juice.

Juice hopped out, followed by Two-Tall. While Juice was trying to hide the bag under some clothes, Two-Tall put two in his head, dropping his body on the curb.

Chapter 17

It was a rainy Friday afternoon outside, and the rain was just beginning to clear up. Jimmy had about twenty of his men strategically positioned on the dock with high-powered artillery, waiting on the shipment of a thousand kilos of uncut powder, a hundred kilos of heroin, a thousand pounds of hydro, and a million X pills to arrive. Two bulletproof Mercedes Sprinter vans waited patiently at the top of the dock while the men kept their eyes open for any unwanted authorities.

Jimmy paid all the workers at the port to mind their own business, so their ship would pull up at any time.

McDuffy, being the underboss, did a perimeter check with everyone. He had men positioned on cranes, in offices, in cars, and even in the water.

A few minutes later, McDuffy spotted the ship as it was pulling up to the dock with their shipment, heading toward them. "Here we go!" McDuffy said, smiling while rubbing his hands together.

The minute the ship stopped, the workers went to work, putting crates into the vans.

Earlier that day, McDuffy had the real shipment put into two other vans. That way, if the authorities showed up, they wouldn't be getting anything but flour, grass, and fake, crushed-up pills.

"We about to see millions!" McDuffy told Music.

Music just nodded. He didn't think they were making the right choice by stealing the shipment from Jimmy.

"We have passports to get the fuck out of the state! We'll dump the shipment for cheap and then go overseas and be kings!" McDuffy said.

Music nodded again, and then the two just smiled.

Meanwhile, the fake shipment had made it to the rendezvous spot safely. The two vans drove right into the warehouse, where Jimmy was standing, puffing on a Newport, waiting. The men hopped out of the vans and then unloaded the crates. When Jimmy ordered them to bust one of the crates open, everyone stared in shock at the contents inside, wondering what had gone wrong.

Jimmy fumingly threw his Newport on the ground.

"Open the others," he said, walking up to another one.

When the worker opened it up and saw grass, they knew someone was going to die.

Jimmy pulled his 9mm out. "Does anyone wanna tell me what the hell happened to my shit?" he yelled with spit flying out of his mouth.

The workers nervously let their heads drop as Jimmy stared at them, breathing heavily. Then one of the workers looked up and around and saw that McDuffy and Music weren't amongst the group. "Where's McDuffy and Music?" He asked the men.

They all shrugged their shoulders. Then it dawned on Jimmy that McDuffy was the one who put all this together, and Music was just supposed to keep his eyes on him.

"Y'all telling me that my own fucking men, McDuffy and Music, are behind this bullshit?" Jimmy asked the workers.

"Yes, sir," he said.

"Find them right now!" he yelled with veins popping out of his forehead.

Everyone hopped into the vans and headed out to find McDuffy and Music.

***

McDuffy pulled into the back of his baby momma's crib. He hopped out of the van and busted one crate open, loading the kilos into a duffle bag to make a few thousand quickly. He only took ten of them.

Both of their phones were blowing up nonstop.

"They already know we did it!" Music said.

"Shut the hell up and get in!" McDuffy told him.

After Music hopped in the van, McDuffy pulled off and headed to the crib he'd rented in 2-6. Jimmy never knew McDuffy grew up in Indianapolis as a kid. He was from 2-6 until his mom moved out of town. They were going to lie low until they moved some kilos.

On the other side of town, Jimmy's low-level workers were on the hunt to find McDuffy and Music. They were using all the connections they had. Both of their cribs were empty. The workers went to all their families, bitches, or friends' cribs, slapping them around for whatever info they had.

Meanwhile, Jimmy was at his store, smoking excessively. He'd smoked his tenth Newport.

It was over $40 million. If he didn't recover this shipment, he would be out of millions. He'd been too relaxed and off his square. He had to tighten his game back right. The old him would have seen this shit coming.

"Mr. Jimmy, are you alright?" his wife, Savannah, asked, ready to go out and put a whole clip into someone's head.

While they were at work, she called him mister, so no one would think she was the shit. She took running a business to heart.

Jimmy waved her off. He just wanted everyone to leave him alone with his own thoughts. He hadn't eaten one meal since learning that McDuffy and Music backdoored him. Jimmy's phone rang. He picked up, thinking it was news about McDuffy and Music.

"Hello?" he picked up.

"What time can I pull up?" Uno asked.

Jimmy shook his head as he inhaled and exhaled.

"We have big problems. It seems McDuffy and Music ran off with the shipment."

"Those bitch ass niggas!" Uno cursed, wondering how this was going to affect his team and their money.

"Don't trip. Your money is insured," Jimmy told him.

"How can me and my team be a hand?" Uno asked.

"Just keep your eyes and ears to the streets, and let me know if anyone is dumping fish, hydro, X-pills, and I know there's not many selling heroin," Jimmy said.

"Just give me a few days, and if things don't pan out right, I got you."

"Listen, Jimmy. We're family now, so you're not alone out here, feel me? I'm gonna put word out to my team right away," Uno assured him. Uno had put Jimmy in a good mood.

"Thank you, Uno. I love you like family, too!"

Uno's phone beeped. "Love. I got another call coming in. I'll call you ASAP," he said, then clicked over. "Hello?" he picked up.

"Hey, baby, just calling to say love you," Punkin said.

"I love you, too. Where's my other baby at?" he asked.

"She's right here. Say something to her," Punkin said, holding the phone for their daughter.

"Daddy love you, baby," Uno said into the phone.

"I love you, Dada," she replied.

"Anyway, what you up to?" Punkin asked.

"Me, LR, and Nasty just left from signing the real estate deeds.

"Okay, call me later. I love you," she said.

"Love you too," he replied before they hung up.

***

McDuffy peeped out the hotel curtains when he heard a car pull up in the parking lot. "It's him," he told Music as he gave him the nod while he stood behind the door with his gun. Hip-Hop knocked on the door, and McDuffy unlocked the locks, letting him in.

"What's up, cuz?" McDuffy said.

"What it do, big cuz?" Hip-Hop responded with dap. Music looked at the two with crazy looks, not understanding the two saying 'cuz'.

McDuffy turned around and smiled. "What that look for? Yeah, this my cousin. You see, I been putting this plan together for a while, and when you agreed, I knew I had him," McDuffy said. McDuffy went over to the bed and opened a duffle bag with twenty-five kilos inside. He handed one to Hip-Hop.

"I want $10,000 a kilo upfront and $15,000 if I got to front it to you," McDuffy said.

"How y'all get all this—" Hip-Hop attempted to ask, but McDuffy put his hand up.

"Don't ask no fucking questions!"

"Coo'," Hip-Hop said, nodding his head.

"Just give me six of them upfront so I can let my people see what the shit be like," Hip-Hop said.

McDuffy put the six inside Hip-Hop's bag. "You have three days tops," he told him.

"That's what's up," Hip-Hop said, walking toward the door.

"Bring our cash the next time you pull up!" McDuffy told him.

McDuffy and Music waited a few minutes to let Hip-Hop get away before they walked out, then hopped in the van, heading back to their safe spot.

On the way back, they drove in silence. Music was thinking about the consequences they were going to have for stealing, while McDuffy was thinking about how he was going to spend his money.

As soon as Hip-Hop left, Black's trap was the first stop he made on his list. Black immediately dropped the cash for the six for $17,000 apiece and then placed an order for another six. Hip-Hop let him know that he wasn't able to do shit until the next morning. Then he headed to his crib, ending the night on a good note with a $42,000 profit.

Chapter 17

The next morning, bright and early, Hip-Hop called McDuffy and told him that he needed to pull up on him. The two agreed to meet at the same spot. After hanging up with McDuffy, Hip-Hop thought about how he was going to convince Black to give him the money for the six now. That way, he would come up on top with him paying $10,000 a brick instead of $15,000. He called Black when an idea popped into his mind.

Twenty minutes later, Hip-Hop was parked in front of Black's spot in Anderson, waiting for Black to arrive. He had Black thinking he was copping six himself too, but if they went in together, they could get a better deal, and Black went for it.

Black's Cadillac Escalade pulled up behind Hip-Hop's Ram truck. Business had kind of started booming again for Black since opening a few new spots.

When Juice got killed, he had to put some new young dudes to work. After surveying the block, Black hopped out with a bag and got into Hip-Hop's truck. Hip-Hop tried not to show how anxious he was to get the bag out of Black's hands.

"I'm not gonna to play with you about my bread," Black said with an earnest face.

"Shit, nigga, I'm trying to help you keep a few bands in your pocket. I don't have to let you in, but I fucks with you!" Hip-Hop said.

"Just hurry up with my shit!" Black said, hopping out, leaving the bag in the seat.

Hip-Hop cheerfully honked his horn and drove off with a smile on his face. He turned up Big Tymers 'Big Ballin' and headed to the meeting spot to meet his cousin McDuffy. Hip-Hop arrived at the hotel promptly at one o'clock. He held up two bags of money and said, "Look what I got for y'all."

McDuffy peeped around the corner nervously before shutting the door behind Hip-Hop.

"How much bread you bring us?" Music asked.

Hip-Hop threw him one bag.

"That's the $90,000 I owed y'all!" He threw McDuffy the other bag. "And that's another $102,000 for twelve more bricks," he said with a sinister grin.

McDuffy handed the other bag to Music to make sure everything was good.

"That's what's up, cuz," McDuffy told Hip-Hop, nodding his head. "I hope you didn't sell any of those to that bitch ass Uno, did you?"

"Man, fuck that nigga, Uno! I hate that nigga guts as much as you!" Hip-Hop said, smiling. "What I did was sell them to Black since they been beefing, so I'm lookin' at it like Uno can't compare to him."

McDuffy just nodded. "That was a good chess move! You know his archenemy should be able to corner the market. After Music verified that the count was on point, he nodded to McDuffy.

McDuffy surprised Hip-Hop by fronting him an additional three bricks for $20,000. The two dapped hands, then Hip-Hop exited the hotel with a smile and headed back to Anderson.

In Anderson, Black was on cloud nine after talking to Hip-Hop. He had just come back from checking on his spots, and business was booming at every last one. Not to mention, he was making two bricks out of one.

Hip-Hop pulled up to Black's trap, parked behind Black, and then hopped in the truck with him.

"What's the word?" Black asked.

Hip-Hop nodded at the bag sitting on the floor. He handed the bag to Black, who unzipped it.

"Why it's eight of them in here?" Black asked.

"I got a deal from my people. I just dipped into my bankroll and went ahead and copped a few more," Hip-Hop lied. "I'm about to dip out for a few days, so I put the two in there because I know you may need them, feel me," Hip-Hop said.

"How much you want for the extra ones?" Black asked.

Hip-Hop smiled. "Since I fucks with you, just give me $25,000!"

***

Black had a few little niggas in Nap still keeping eyes on Uno and his team. He told them if they had any openings to take the shot, but no news had come through yet.

***

The properties Uno, LR, and Nasty invested in were in good shape. Everything was almost done. They all planned to keep flipping properties. The assets that Big Dawg left him were really going to help him clean up all the dirty money.

As Uno cruised toward Punkin's friend's shop, he thought about how she had been pushing him to leave the game. She supported him, and then she wanted what she wanted.

'What the fuck is wrong with this girl?' Uno wondered, noticing the look on Punkin's face as he pulled into the parking lot of the shop.

Punkin tried to act like everything was cool as she walked toward the car.

"What's up, baby? What's wrong with you?" he asked as she dropped into her seat.

Punkin just sat there, and tears started pouring down her face.

"Baby, what's up?" he asked empathetically, knowing something was really going on. He pulled out into traffic.

Punkin turned her face so Uno could see the side of her face. He hit the brakes when he saw the handprint on her face. "Who the fuck did that?" he asked, grabbing her face with fire behind his eyes.

"Some dude and female claiming to be friends with Black said it's a message for you," she said.

Uno pulled off down the street. He stopped at the light. Meanwhile, the people Black had watching Uno were right behind them, following them down the street.

"I'm going to need you to drive past them so I can see what Uno look like."

Uno got on the highway, headed out west, and Black's people continued to follow.

A few minutes later, they were both flying, doing sixty-five miles per hour on the highway. Traffic was slowing down, and she thought she was hitting the brakes, but ended up mashing the gas.

"Oh, shit!" Uno screamed, trying to move out of the car's way that he saw coming in the rearview mirror, but the car slammed into them. "Fuck!" Uno yelled as the impact flipped the car over twice.

Unfortunately, Punkin wasn't wearing her seatbelt, so the impact bounced her body all around the car. When the car finally stopped, Uno immediately unfastened his seatbelt and checked on Punkin's well-being.

"Hell naw!" he cried, seeing Punkin lying unconscious on the back seat with blood dripping from her face. His first thought was to pull his 9mm out and empty the clip into whoever it was that hit them, but hearing the sirens changed his mind. Plus, Punkin's health was more important. He had to get rid of his gun, so he hit a few buttons, and a stash spot popped out.

When the little nigga hopped out of their car, he and Uno locked eyes. The two looked at each other for a second. Uno tried to figure out where he knew his face from until it dawned on him that this was all Black's plan.

"I got you," Uno commented, then looked at the dead girl behind the wheel. Uno watched the dude disappear, knowing he and Black had limited time.

***

Every news station was out live on the scene of the accident. The dude's face was on every channel as a person of interest. According to the people who were on the highway, he intentionally caused the accident.

Uno was nervously sitting in the emergency room, praying that everything went well with Punkin's surgery. He had put word out to shut down their operation until Black was caught. His $150,000 reward had the whole city on a manhunt for him. Uno was determined to find Black and kill him and his team.

A couple of hours later, Uno rushed Punkin's surgeon when he entered the room. Uno held his breath while trying to read his expression.

"She was beaten up pretty badly. She's in a coma right now. It's up to her at this point," the surgeon told him. "Sir, are you okay?" the surgeon asked, seeing that Uno's face turned red.

"May I see her?" he asked.

"Yes, she's in the ICU."

Uno gathered himself together, then stood up and shook the surgeon's hand.

"Thank you, doc," he said.

"I wish you well," the surgeon said before excusing himself from the room.

The long, cold hallway leading to the ICU gave Uno goosebumps. Every room he passed, he heard beeping sounds coming from the machines. When Uno reached Punkin's room, he had to take a couple of minutes before he entered.

Punkin's mother was sitting bedside, holding her hand, while LR sat around the room. LR looked up at him, speechless as he stood in the doorway.

"Are you okay, son?" Punkin's mother surprisingly asked.

He just nodded his head as he felt relieved that she spoke to him. Seeing Punkin in the condition she was in hit home, and tears fell from his eyes. At that moment, he knew she was his heart. He walked up to the bed and grabbed her hand, leaned over, and kissed her lips.

"Baby, I'm sorry, and I want you to know you need to come back to me and our daughter. I'll be back later, but I gotta go out and handle something," he said, then kissed her goodbye on the lips again.

LR stood up, ready to follow Uno's lead. "Murrell and Rodney, don't be going out there starting anything," Punkin and LR's mother said before they walked out of the room.

Neither one was trying to hear anything anyone had to say as they continued to walk out of the room.

"I put $150,000 out here for Black," Uno told LR.

"I just put $100,000 out there to my little people, too."

Uno pulled out his phone and hit Nasty up.

"Tell Mo-Mo, Lil' E, Tezzy, and Babyface that I upped the reward to $350,000," he said when Nasty picked up. Then he hung up.

With $350,000 on Black's and his crew's heads, the city went nuts. They were receiving calls left and right.

How the hell did they get Punkin caught up in this mess?

Chapter 18

Uno was on Nasty's sofa, still asleep, when he walked into his living room with LR behind him. Nasty grabbed the sheet and pulled it off of him.

"Bitch, get up!" Nasty said.

"What time is it?" Uno asked in a groggy voice.

"It's four thirty, nigga! Me and LR done went out and handled our business, had lunch with some friends, came back, and yo' ass still in here sleep on the sofa!" Nasty said.

Uno had been at Nasty's house ever since that stuff happened to Punkin. He couldn't go home without Punkin being there, for some reason.

"Bro, you need to get the fuck up out of this house and go handle your business. Sis is strong, so it's just a matter of days, feel me?" LR said.

"Y'all right about that," Uno said, then walked into Nasty's closet to grab a fit to get dressed and showered for the day.

Twenty minutes later, they were heading back to the city.

***

All of Uno's and the WSF's spots had slowed down drastically. A lot of people who had fronted the last of the work were just finishing up. After making their rounds, Uno shot over to Muncie to see the status of Jimmy.

While headed there, they contemplated their next move. One thing was for sure that they needed to get the people that they had lost back on board. They were hoping Jimmy had some good news for them. Word around town was that Hip-Hop was now the nigga to see if you wanted some bricks.

Twenty minutes later, Uno pulled into the store lot and parked. They all hopped out and headed inside. Savannah greeted Uno with a hug when he walked into the store.

"How you doing, sexy?" she asked.

"How you doing? Where's your husband?" Uno asked.

"At his spot," she replied.

They headed to the back of the store.

"Here he is!" Jimmy stood and said when Uno walked into his office.

The two embraced, and then all four of them sat down.

"Still no word on either of those dudes?" Uno asked.

"Still nothing," Jimmy said, pathetically shaking his head.

Today would mark a week and half since McDuffy and Music had cut out with his shipment.

"You know. We not tripping. You can keep that bread," LR offered, with Uno and Nasty nodding their heads.

Jimmy waved them off, declining. "Nah, then I'll be more in the hole."

Uno studied Jimmy's face. He could see the street taking its toll. The loss was really messing with Jimmy. He didn't look like himself.

"Are you good?" Uno asked, concerned.

Jimmy fumingly hit his fist on the desk. "Nah, I can't let this pass, because then all I have done over these years wouldn't be nothing in the eyes of the people that know me. It's not about the money or dope with me. I want them two heads on a platter. I'll pay $1 million right now to whoever brings me those two bitches!" he said.

"What?" Uno asked with his eyebrow raised.

LR looked at Nasty, who smiled in turn.

"Where I'm from, a man's respect means more than money! Money is worthless without respect! Right now, in the street's eyes, I look weak," he frowned and said.

Uno placed his hand on his shoulder and replied, "Not to us." He pointed at all three of them.

"Savannah has a bag for you. I'm sorry I had to give it back," Jimmy said.

Heated, all three stood up. "As of today, I'm officially putting all my connections together to find them two and this dude Black," Uno said.

***

Back in the city, Hip-Hop was really starting to feel himself. In the last week, he had brought McDuffy over $1 million and a profit of over $300,000 in cash for himself. That was the most money he'd ever had in his life. The money was pouring in so fast that if business kept going like that, he'd be at $1 million in no time.

Hip-Hop drove through the streets with a newfound attitude. He was just leaving Black's spot after grabbing another $200,000 from his for another eleven bricks. That alone was going to be a $94,000 profit, let alone a few dudes whose money he had that he was charging $20,000 a brick.

Hip-Hop smiled. Life was good. He was on his way to get on.

***

McDuffy and Music were just waking up after partying all night with two females they had picked up from the bar. McDuffy had made a big scene last night, buying out the bar. While McDuffy was having the time of his life, Music was trying to come up with a plan to get back in with Jimmy without getting killed. He thought about calling Uno, but had to think about how he would react.

McDuffy got up and grabbed his phone to check it. Seeing he had missed Hip-Hop's call, he called him back.

"Hello?" Hip-Hop picked up.

"Yeah?" McDuffy asked.

"I need to see you," Hip-Hop said.

"Same place, eight tonight," McDuffy replied, then hung up.

***

After making his rounds, Uno cruised the city, trying to figure out where Hip-Hop was getting all of this dope from that he'd been moving. He just came up out of the blue. He was just coming from hollering at a few of his people from 49th, and even they had told him that they had just spent their money with Hip-Hop. Uno was growing agitated. That nigga was really starting to show his ass.

'Damn, who the hell is he fucking with to the point he can unload bricks for $17,000 apiece?' Uno thought.

"Hello?" he picked up

"Hey, I'm just getting home. I have that ready for you," Savannah stated.

"How was your man doing when you left?" Uno asked.

"I couldn't get him to eat or do anything. The loss really hurt him. A portion of this is on me, too," she said.

"How?" Uno wanted to know.

"Because I should have known something was goin' on by how the way McDuffy was moving. I don't know how Music got into it with McDuffy, because he was a loyal person," she said.

"Well, I be there soon," Uno said, hanging up. An hour later, Uno was pulling up to the address Savannah texted him. He rang the doorbell and waited.

Savannah opened the door, wearing a robe. Uno tried not to look at her body, but to be an older lady, she was killing some of the young girls in the body department.

"Come in," she said, moving to the side.

Uno looked around the house at all the art on the way. "Y'all have a nice house," he told her, following behind her, trying not to look at how her ass was moving.

"Thank you. This just one of the places we got," she told him, heading toward the bar.

"Do you want a drink, Uno?" she asked him.

"Yeah, please," he said, sitting on the sofa.

"So that bag is yours by the door," she said, crossing her leg, showing off her thick thighs.

Uno looked away as his dick jumped in his pants. She saw the print and just smiled.

"Let's not play games, Uno. I know you like what you see. Don't put all your trust in my husband. Where he's from, blacks would always be under him, and if you get too big, he will start playing games. He told me Big Dawg was your brother. Now, that was a man before his time. Anyway, I want and need some dick," she said, standing and dropping the robe.

"Naw, I can't," Uno tried to get up but fell back on the sofa. His head started spinning a little, and his eyes shut.

Twenty minutes later, Uno could barely open his eyes, but when he did, Savannah was riding his dick, moaning. It felt so good that he started gripping her ass.

"Yes, that's what I'm talking about." She moaned in his ear. "Beat this pussy up, please, Uno."

Uno pumped harder and harder until he felt he was about to cum. A few minutes later, they both nutted.

"This is my dick now," she said, then kissed him on the cheek before leaving the room.

Uno grabbed the bag and shot out the door, heading back to his spot. As soon as he got in the car, his phone rang. "Hello?' he picked up.

"This Uno?" the voice asked.

"Yeah. What's good?" he asked.

"Naw, before I break something down to you, I want you to put it on your daughter you not going to do nothing besides pull up," the voice said.

"Coo'," Uno said, not promising anything.

"This is Music, and I'm going to text you the address where everything is and where we are, but I need you to get me back good with Jimmy, please," Music said.

Uno almost crashed as he sat up in his seat.

"What you just say?" Uno asked.

Music broke everything down to him again.

Chapter 19

It was seven thirty that evening, and Uno had left the hospital not too long before after sitting with Punkin.

Thirty minutes later, Uno parked across the street from the address Music texted him just in time to see Hip-Hop pulling into the parking lot of the hotel. Uno just sat patiently, observing everything from across the street. He watched Hip-Hop cheerfully hop out of the car with a duffle bag. He knocked on the last door, and the room door opened.

Uno watched McDuffy step out of the room, survey the area, and then head back inside. Uno quickly pulled his phone out and called LR and Nasty.

"What's good?" LR answered, guiding his lady friend's head up and down on his dick.

"Hold on," Uno said, clicking Nasty in.

"I need y'all to get booted and meet me over by the mall," Uno said with urgency behind his voice.

LR sat up in his seat and motioned for his lady friend to stop. "I got you, bro!" he said, then hung up.

"I'm down the street," Nasty said, hanging up.

Uno pressed a few buttons, and his back seat flipped down. He grabbed his vest and then twisted his silencer onto his pistol. He slid his .380 into his ankle holster, tucked his twin Glock .45 caliber in his shoulder holster, and waited for his brothers to show up.

Nasty pulled up in the mall parking lot. He hit Uno to let him know where he was. Twenty minutes passed, and Hip-Hop was still inside the room.

LR called back. "What up, my nigga? Where y'all at?" LR asked when Uno picked up.

Uno explained everything, gave LR his location, and then told him it was subject to change. LR let him know that he was five minutes away before the two hung up. LR was speeding, trying to get to their location. It was a good thing he was already in the city, or else it would've taken him longer to reach them. The Porsche truck engine roared as LR fearlessly weaved in and out of lanes to rush to his partner's assistance.

Five minutes later, Hip-Hop emerged from the room. McDuffy and Music followed. After they cautiously surveyed the area for any suspicious cars, Hip-Hop hopped in his car, while McDuffy and Music jumped in the van.

"Come on, bro. Where you at?" Uno impatiently waited for LR's arrival.

LR was two blocks away at a stoplight. As soon as it turned green, the Porsche's engine peaked out as he floored it. LR pulled out his phone to call Uno. Hip-Hop had just pulled off, and McDuffy was backing out of the parking lot when Uno's phone chirped.

"Yeah!" he answered as he cranked up the car.

"I'm here! Where y'all at!" LR yelled over the roaring engine.

After Uno let him know where he was, LR disconnected and got to the right part.

Meanwhile, Uno pulled out of the parking lot and followed behind McDuffy.

Uno saw the headlights from LR's truck heading their way.

"The green van. Block it. So get in front so we can box him in."

LR gripped the steering wheel, mashed the gas, and pulled in front of the van, making McDuffy stop the van.

Uno and Nasty pulled up behind them, and Uno texted Music to let him know it was them.

McDuffy's eyes popped out of his face when he looked over and saw Music's pistol in his face.

"Put your hands up, bitch," Music said.

Uno, Nasty, and LR quickly hopped out of their vehicles, extracted McDuffy from the van, and dragged a screaming McDuffy over to Uno's car.

"Here! Put this nigga in the trunk!" Uno said, knocking McDuffy out.

"Nasty, jump in the van and follow me," Uno said, hopping back into his car with Music.

Uno whipped out his phone and called Jimmy as he sped through back roads.

Jimmy's phone just rang. Uno's heart was beating from the rush. He felt like he just did some James Bond shit.

"Hello?" Jimmy answered in a sleepy voice on the fifth ring.

"Are you ready to eat them platters?"

Jimmy sat up. He sat on the edge of the bed, flicked on the nightlight, and gave Uno an address where he could meet him.

After the two hung up, Uno headed to the destination. He looked in his rearview mirror and saw Nasty right behind him. He just smiled as he put in his Boosie CD and got his mind right to put in work.

***

McDuffy found himself inside a warehouse tied to a chair when he regained consciousness from the knockout.

"How you be, McDuffy?" Uno taunted with a grin. "Surely, you didn't think you was gonna get away with the bitch shit you pulled?" Uno asked, then ferociously hit him in the mouth, knocking his chair over. He kicked him in the face a few times.

Jimmy and his men were just walking into the warehouse.

"Sorry for getting started without you, guys," Uno said. "Before you do anything, let me explain something to you. McDuffy was plotting to rob you, and he been hitting Hip-Hop with bricks, letting him get them off for $10,000 up front and $15,000 if he front them to him. We got the whole shipment and over $1.5 million in cash. How I got this info was by him," Uno said, nodding to Music.

Jimmy reached for his waist.

"Wait, Jimmy." Uno's hand rose up like a stop sign. "I believe him when he says he was on your team the whole time, so give him five minutes."

Music breathed a sigh of relief. Hoping for a reprieve, he said, "Jimmy, I know you may not believe me, but when McDuffy came to me with the plan, it was my plan to come to you, but I wanted to see who else McDuffy had on his team. He been hitting Hip-Hop with bricks, who, in return, was selling them to someone named Black."

"Say that name again," Uno prompted.

"Black. All the other drugs is there, and I didn't spend not a dollar. I have video of McDuffy and Hip-Hop talking every time."

Jimmy walked up to McDuffy and stared into his eyes. "Your bitch ass thought you could steal from me and get away with it?" he yelled.

"I need you to get Hip-Hop online," Uno said.

Music grabbed McDuffy's phone and texted and told him he had something for him, so pull up to the address.

Twenty minutes later, Hip-Hop was knocking on the door. One of the workers opened the door. Hip-Hop's smile turned into a frown when he saw all the guns in his face.

***

"You know. In the morning, you two are gonna be famous," Uno said, pacing in front of McDuffy and Hip-Hop. "Really, y'all should thank us. McDuffy, I was goin' to kill your family, but I'm goin' to let them do them. But the sister of yours? I have to see what them guts about. And you, Hip-Hop, I will let you walk out if you tell me where Black is."

"All I know is he has a few spots in Anderson. He calls me." Hip-Hop knew he was dead.

"Okay, let's get down to business." Uno walked over and kneeled in front of McDuffy. His dick got hard, seeing the fear in his eyes. Tools in his hand, he grabbed McDuffy's balls and raised his eyebrow. "Looks like I got you by the balls now." Uno looked McDuffy in the eyes and then castrated him.

"Ahhh!" He screamed as blood gushed out of where his sex organs once were.

Nasty and LR stood with their faces twisted. Uno was sick! His crazy ass was smiling, looking McDuffy in the eyes.

"Please. No. No. No!" Hip-Hop shook his head and pleaded as Uno walked toward him.

Uno stood before Hip-Hop, laughing at the fear. He did the same thing to him that he did to McDuffy.

"Ahhh!" Hip-Hop leaned forward and yelled.

"Bro, why you didn't just shoot the niggas?" LR asked.

"That would have been too easy for me. Plus, we sending a message for all to hear," Uno replied as he stood in a puddle of blood.

Uno grabbed their nuts and penises, then placed them in a bag.

"What the fuck are we gonna do with them?" Nasty asked.

Chapter 20

Around eight o'clock the next morning, dozens of officers from different agencies swarmed the crime scene where McDuffy and Hip-Hop's bodies were found. Without a strong stomach or already being used to this type of thing, a person would've vomited all over themselves like a few officers had already done.

A housekeeper making her rounds found the two in the hotel room. Sean had been working homicide for over twenty years, and it was by far one of the most horrendous murders he'd ever seen.

"We're definitely ruling this one drug-related. They found over $10,000 in cash and half a brick of cocaine on the table."

Cameras flashed as McDuffy and Hip-Hop lay in separate beds with their dicks superglued in their ass and testicles hanging out of their mouths. There was writing on the wall in blood that read: We bitches, so we don't need our dicks and love sucking shit. We fucked ourselves when we crossed the wrong people! And there was a *Wild* Uno playing card stuck on the wall with blood.

Sean shook his head when he read the message.

Back at the store, Jimmy smoked his Newport, happy with the headlines on the news. Not only had McDuffy and Hip-Hop murders made the headlines, but they were on every channel. He shook his head as he thought about how Uno and his team made everything happen. He was glad to be working with him and not against him. Jimmy decided to hit him up.

Uno was chilling in the recliner next to Punkin's bed, watching the news. Mugshots of McDuffy and Hip-Hop flashed on the screen. His phone beeped, letting him know someone was trying to reach him about some business.

"Hello?" he answered.

"A standing ovation," was all Jimmy said.

***

Black sat in front of his television, nursing the drink in his hand. He couldn't believe someone killed Hip-Hop. He was glad he still had bricks put up. Now he had to slow walk it until he found another plug or when Man-Man let him know all was well on his end. But when the news showed the Uno card, it dawned on him—Uno and WSF were behind the murders. That was a clear message.

Uno was really applying pressure to try and get him to surface. Uno's bounty had made it impossible for him to walk in the city. He was shitty because he hadn't come up with a plan to get Uno out of the way. He sprinkled salt and pepper on his food, stirred it, then started eating.

Meanwhile, a shooter was calmly sitting outside of Black's spot in a black Kia, listening to everything going on inside the trap, thanks to the bug the dope sting dropped in the house. Everybody in the house started choking on their food. He calmly eased out of the truck, wearing his gloves. He picked the locks of the back door and eased inside.

Black and two of his men were lying on the floor.

***

Uno was awakened out of his dream when the nurse walked into Punkin's room, making her rounds. He spent another night at Punkin's bedside, hoping she would wake up out of her coma. Pooder had been asking when she could come home, and it hurt Uno that he couldn't give her a day. Uno stood up and went to the restroom so the nurse could do her job.

Uno's phone rang. "Hello?" he answered.

"I have that package you been looking for," the caller said.

"Who is this?" Uno asked, rushing out of the bathroom.

"Just do you still want that person for that $350,000?" the caller asked.

"Yeah, my offer stands," Uno replied, hoping this was a real caller.

The caller told him he would text an address and to meet later.

***

The address the caller texted was a deserted warehouse located south of the city. Uno had all his men all over the land of the warehouse just in case this was some bullshit. LR, Nasty, and the BTG followed behind Uno as they entered the dark enclosure with a duffle bag with the money inside.

"Yo," Uno said, his voice echoing throughout the warehouse. No one answered. Shielding Uno, LR and BTG scanned the area like marksmen with their guns drawn. Nobody in the crew believed this person had Black. Everyone in the city had been looking for this nigga for days now.

"Something is funny," LR said.

Everyone got tense when they heard a door opening and the sound of footsteps walking through puddles of water, growing closer. LR and the BTG had their guns pointed in the direction from which the footsteps were coming.

"Are we going to do this or what?" Uno asked.

"Did you bring the money?" a dark shadow appeared and asked.

"I got the bread. The thing is, did you bring him with you?" Uno asked.

"Open the bag," the shadow said.

Uno unzipped the bag and opened it so he could see all the money. "Okay, you see the money. Now let me see him."

Everyone's eyes popped when the shadow flashed his light on Black's face.

While Uno's blood boiled. He was ready to get his hands on Black.

"Who do you work for?" Uno asked.

"I work for myself but sometimes with my other family," the shadow replied.

Uno threw the duffle bag over to where he assumed the shadow was standing.

"Hand that bitch over!" Uno said, and the shadow reached down and grabbed the bag. "I have to admit, you're good! I can see myself in you, and for some reason, I feel connected to you!"

The shadow laughed. "I think we are in many ways than one," the shadow said.

Uno and his crew looked at each other, puzzled.

The shadow made himself visible. Uno laughed as he looked at his cousin Baby J.

"Nigga, what it do?" Uno hugged him tight.

"Shit, cuz, I been watching you from a distance, so you know I had to get dude," Baby J said.

Chapter 21

The private jet landed smoothly and on time at the airstrip in Mexico. Inside the airplane were Man-Man and Two-Tall. They were in Mexico to meet up with the king of Mexico, Jimmy. As they walked down the stairs, Man-Man's heart started beating fast because he knew he was so close to putting all his pieces in order. He looked over at Two-Tall, and relief swept over him, causing his heart to stop racing. Man-Man knew he was standing next to a solid individual who had his back.

Neither one had ever been to Mexico before, but as they took in the scenery, they regretted not having come before, because it was breathtaking. Not only was the land beautiful, but so were its inhabitants. People stood around everywhere, selling stuff, talking, riding bikes, looking happy and carefree as if everything in the world were peaches and cream.

Sitting in the back of the black Mercedes truck Jimmy had sent for them, they rode quietly through Mexico's streets. In a matter of minutes, the once-beautiful scenery transformed right before their eyes. They both looked at the narrow streets, dilapidated houses, and buildings, and were amazed as they took in the sight, because neither of them knew that Mexico had urban neighborhoods.

As the scenery changed once again into nice homes, the truck slowed down before turning onto a pathway that led to the most beautiful house that they'd ever seen. The huge mansion sat almost on a block of land. The shrubbery surrounding the house was rows of trees and flowers. The driveway resembled a car dealership, with Mercedes, Lexus, Bentley, Ferrari, and Aston Martin cars parked there.

Jimmy wasn't playing. He had young shooters armed with AK-47s walking around. Every last man had the same mean stare, but that didn't faze them.

"Come on," Man-Man said as he forced the door open. Two-Tall got out, still in awe of the house that stood before them.

"Welcome to my house," Jimmy said as he opened the front door of the house.

Man-Man and Two-Tall's heads were fucked up behind it. They knew he got money, but by the looks of it, he was the boss of the bosses. Jimmy gave them a tour of the house, which blew their minds. He showed them all ten bedrooms, ten bathrooms, two kitchens, a six-car garage, and more.

Making it back downstairs, they all took a seat at the table. A butler came out to serve them drinks.

"After they killed Red, and you did that Punkin job, I told you to be patient, and I got you. I'm a man of my word, as I believe you already know," Jimmy says.

"I really feel played. You over here sitting back like a king, when I'm in the states, fucked up," Man-Man said.

"Don't feel that way. I just wanted to wait for the perfect time to bring you into my world. I had to see who you really were. I saw the power you possess with the young boys back in the States. I wanted you to understand the power you had before showing my hand to you. Now that you understand the power that lays in your hand and see the type of power I have, what are y'all trying to do?" Jimmy asked.

Man-Man looked at Two-Tall, and together, they both said, "We want the whole city."

"Is that all? When you can have your hands on the whole Midwest? But we will take baby steps," Jimmy said.

"Come. Let me show y'all something," Jimmy said, getting up from the table. "So, you both ready to really get this money?" Jimmy asked, looking at them to see if they were really ready to step their game up.

"Hell yeah. We ain't new to getting money. All we need is the dope, and the city is ours," Man-Man said.

"Since Uno and LR got locked up, the rest of the crew just been laying back, giving other crews time to build up. They once had a hold of the city, but with so many different crews now opening up shop, it will be hard for them. We have a few youngsters that's ready to put in that work as we speak," Man-Man said.

"You don't have to worry about Uno or LR, because they done for. I have an inside scoop, so just worry about getting this money," Jimmy said, walking into the kitchen. He stopped at the security monitors he had on the wall and pointed at his companion, who lay curled up in a fetal position with her hands tucked between her legs.

Music walked into the kitchen and shook his head at Jimmy. He didn't like how Jimmy had been having his companion locked away in a room for as long as he had, and no one knew of her but a handful of people.

Looking at her beauty made Jimmy's dick rock up. As he talked, he unlocked the door and began to walk down the stairs.

His companion heard footsteps descending the stairs, so she pretended to be asleep. She didn't know how long she'd been stuck down in the room, but the last memory was of her walking into the house, and everything went black.

"Wake up, sleeping beauty. I want you to see someone," Jimmy said, shaking the bed she lay on.

To the naked eye, the room was like a small apartment. It had a flat-screen TV on the wall, carpet running throughout the room, a queen-size bed, cable, and its own private restroom.

When the woman looked up, Man-Man and Two-Tall's minds started racing. The same question popped into both of their minds.

"Is that who I think it is?" Man-Man asked.

Jimmy raised his glass for a toast. Man-Man and Two-Tall reciprocated the gesture. Jimmy spoke. "Here's to all missions. Let's get y'all back to the states so y'all can get what's y'all! Music will make sure the package gets to Indianapolis in the next few days."

Sitting on the jet, chilling, Man-Man and Two-Tall were in their own little thoughts as the plane took off back to Indianapolis.

"I brought you to the table, bro, and introduced you to the plug because we a team, so as soon as we touch, we need to round up as many shooters as we can," Man-Man said.

"No doubt. I understand, fam. Let's get this money," Two-Tall said, giving him dap.

Chapter 22

Man-Man, Two-Tall, and Lipz all sat inside the car, strapping on their vests and making sure their guns were ready.

With Uno, LR, and Nasty out the way, Tezzy and Lil' E had their guard down and began to let other crews get money. They sat down the street from one of Tezzy's and Lil' E's stash spots.

"Everybody in the house get it, but don't touch Trigger," Two-Tall said. There was never any remorse when it came to taking someone's life.

The three exited the car and began to make their way through the back of the houses. As they continued toward the next block, the house popped up. A green drop top, a black Range Rover, and a Ram truck sat in the driveway. They all crept their way up to the house.

"You two, go through the back while I take the front. Trigger just texted and said it's three niggas and a female in the basement," Two-Tall said to Man-Man and Lipz.

The music was blaring throughout the house. Trigger had already unlocked the doors for the crew to enter, so when Two-Tall walked through the front, he saw Man-Man and Lipz entering through the back. The lights inside were all out, so the three moved quickly toward the source of the music. Hearing "Murkin' Season" by Plies put a smile on Two-Tall's face because the song fit right at that moment.

They saw a guy sleeping on the floor, one playing the game on the flat screen, and the other getting ridden by a white girl. Neither the girl nor the dudes knew there were three pairs of eyes watching them.

When the female opened her eyes, she jumped off the dude's dick, making him look at her crazy. Following her eyes, he turned around and saw three people standing over him. Before he could say or do anything, Lipz was on him, slapping him with the butt of the AK-47. This made the others in the room aware.

"Now, we can make this easy or hard. Where's the money and dope?" Man-Man asked, pointing his gun at one of the dude's heads.

"Fuck you, nigga. You a bitch ass dude. Nasty will have y'all head by morning," dude said, smiling.

Boc! Boc!

Lipz put two in his head, dropping his body where he stood. "Now, let's do this again. Where's the money and dope?" Lipz asked.

"I know where everything is, but you have to let me go because I don't have anything to do with this. I was just trying to hustle up some money to feed my two kids," the white girl said, not even fazed by the body that lay at her feet.

"Where is everything? I promise you, you can walk away as long as you promise not to fuck with hoe ass niggas again," Man-Man said.

"I promise. But the money is under the washer, and the dope is under the oven," she said, getting dressed.

Man-Man and Lipz went to where the girl told them, and minutes later, both came back with bags in their hands.

"Good," Two-Tall said, lifting up his 9mm and hitting the two dudes up, then turned toward the white girl who stood, looking him in the eyes.

"No," Man-Man blurted out, surprising himself, Two-Tall, and Lipz.

"You know her?" Two-Tall asked curiously.

"Nah, I don't. She's just in the wrong place at the wrong time. She ain't gotta die," Man-Man told him, not totally sure why he was advocating for the girl.

"A witness is a loose end that might come back to bite you in the ass later, and if it was up to me, I'd kill the bitch, but it's your call. One day, that tender dick shit you be on will get you killed," Two-Tall said, tucking his gun and heading to the door.

Getting back to their stash spot, the three sat at the table and began to count up the money. They had to give Trigger $150,000 for setting up the lick for them. Trigger began to work for the WSF after Uno and LR got locked up and Nasty fell back. He worked his way up from a corner boy to watching over one of their main spots.

"It's $1.3 million here," Man-Man said, only half believing it.

Chapter 23

Nasty read over the message on his phone repeatedly in disbelief. It said they'd been robbed of over $1 million and ten bricks. He felt disrespected. He couldn't breathe as he leaned against his desk. Just $1 million wasn't anything to him. He was just so heated that someone had the balls to touch anything with their stamp on it. This had to be an inside job because everyone knew who ran the city, but what everyone didn't know was that Nasty had spent thousands on surveillance cameras in every spot they had, plus around the neighborhood.

At his main house, he had installed cameras in a three-block radius. To sneak into his crib, one needed a few James Bond agents, and that still might not have been any good. He wasn't a paranoid individual; he just liked to know what was going on around him at all times.

Pulling up the video from the spot that got robbed, Nasty watched three individuals enter the house. Pulling up the basement cameras, he saw Man-Man and two others as face clear as day.

The next night...
Club Ruthie was packed as fuck that night. Bad females surrounded the club. It was a little chilly outside, but that didn't stop the females from wearing next to nothing.

Lil' E pulled up to the club in his brand-new Aston Martin. The car was so sexy that everyone in line couldn't take their eyes off it as he parked. He jumped out, wearing Polo down to his feet while smoking a blunt.

Tezzy pulled up right next to Lil' E's car in a Lamborghini truck.

He jumped out in Prada, looking good.

A G-Wagon pulled into the parking lot at top speed and stopped on the other side of Tezzy's car. Breezy hopped out of the driver's seat in a white Gucci one-piece with the matching pumps. Her friend was killing it too with a black, fitted dress.

Inside Club Ruthie, it was jumping. The DJ had Money Man's single "Boss Up" blasting through the speakers. Niggas wore throwing ones all over the place, just as the females were doing the same. Bad women were all over the floor, popping their asses.

The crowd of partygoers parted like the sea as Tezzy led the way across the room. They could feel eyes on them as they walked through the club. They made it to the stairs that led up to the second floor. The stairwell was dark, but there was a black curtain at the top with a light behind it. When they almost reached the top, a man appeared in front of them. He glanced at them for a few seconds, but he recognized the group. They made their way toward Nasty's office in the back. When they entered the office, they all noticed the lines on his face.

"What's good?" Lil' E asked, being the first to speak.

"Man, just watch this," Nasty said, playing the video. They all took seats around the office as Nasty put the video on the flat screen. As the video began to play, they watched Man-Man and two other people enter their spot and rob it.

"How is it that you two niggas are the bosses out here in the streets, and niggas have the balls to rob the spots? Matter of fact, how the fuck I found out this shit before y'all?" Nasty asked, getting heated all over again.

"I just got back in town late last night," Lil' E said.

"And I been laying low with the kids," Tezzy added.

Chapter 24

Trigger tossed and turned all through the night as he lay next to his son's mother. His eyes popped open as he sat up in bed and looked at the clock on the dresser, which read 3:26 a.m. Getting up, he made his way toward the bathroom that was connected to their bedroom. After Trigger urinated and washed his hands, he looked at himself in the mirror.

Making his way back to bed, he lay back down, closed his eyes, and tried to fall back asleep. Feeling someone standing over him, he opened his eyes to see Nasty sitting in the chair that they had next to the bed. Thinking fast, he tried to sit up but got knocked back down by Lil' E.

Tezzy already had Trigger's baby's momma by the hair, a 9mm in her mouth.

"What the fuck! Why are y'all niggas in my crib?" Trigger asked, trying to sound hard.

Nasty just smiled wickedly at Trigger.

"Where's our money at?" Nasty asked.

"Please! Look! We got robbed! I can make up the money we lost, if this is about the money! I have a little over $100,000 in my stash. Y'all can have it," Trigger said.

"Where?" Nasty asked.

"It's in my son's room in the toy box," he answered.

"Get up." Nasty grabbed Trigger, forcing him out of bed. Making their way into Trigger's son's room, Nasty pointed his gun at his face.

"Where the fuck is it?" Nasty asked, looking at Trigger like he was a lunatic.

Trigger was happy his son had spent the night at his auntie's house because he was sure he and his baby momma were dead. He pulled the toy box out to the middle of the room and dumped all the toys out until he saw the bag that contained the money. He unzipped the bag to show Nasty the money.

Seeing the neat bundles of hundred-dollar bills made Nasty pull the trigger on his gun.

Boc! Boc! Boc!

Nasty let the bullets enter Trigger's face before grabbing the bag. Walking back into the room where Tezzy still had Trigger's baby momma, Nasty gave him the head nod.

"Wait!" she screamed.

"What?" Tezzy asked, ready to take action.

"Man-Man came to him because he been dealing with Trigger sister, and they been plotting and planning on this lick. I overheard Man-Man telling him that they were on some get-back from when y'all took over all their spots. He know where some of y'all spots are, too. Please don't kill me. I also know they hang at Homers in y'all hood," she said, crying.

Tezzy pulled the trigger, splattering her brains all over the wall.

All three disappeared into the night.

***

Lil' E parked on Udell. From where he was parked, he could see the entrance of Club Homers clearly. When Trigger's baby momma informed them that this was one of Man-Man's hangout spots, it made him shitty that they were in the middle of his hood, and he didn't know about it.

Tezzy sat in the driver's seat of the rental. Three cars down sat Lil' E. The club was a few minutes away from closing, which meant they would be coming out.

Lil' E watched the door and saw a few people stepping out in spurts, which let him know the game was about to get started. As he sat back, he rapped the words of Boosie's "Set it Off" song. Finally, he spotted a familiar face from the video.

"Damn." He sighed to himself as the individuals got closer. When he entered the game, he promised himself that he would never harm children or women.

"Fuck it, shit," he said to himself. He didn't start this. 'They initiated it,' he told himself in order to make himself forget the promise he made to himself. As the female stepped within a few feet of the car, the alarm sounded off, and the lights illuminated the area. Lipz's eyes brightened up like quarters. Instead of freezing up, he stood to his feet. As much as he hated to do it, he had no choice because she was on the wrong team.

Boc!

Lil' E fired at her head. She fell backward onto the ground, and he fired a few more times.

Boc! Boc! Boc!

He hit her with every shot.

Lil' E quickly took off into flight toward the waiting car, where Tezzy sat watching the entire show play out. He hopped into the car. His face showed sympathy for the girl. Tezzy looked around, only to see a few people swarming the front door. He quickly sped up the block.

"Fuck!" Lil' E shouted. "Why the fuck did the female from the video have to come out?" he asked sadly. He hated that he had to kill a female, but he knew, had the shoe been on the other foot, she would have gotten him together.

Lipz was the only female in Man-Man's crew, but to the naked eye, she appeared to be a nice looking female, but watching the video, he knew she was a killer.

"I just shot a bitch!" Lil' E said.

"Was she one of theirs?" Tezzy asked.

"It was the one in the video."

"Fuck the bitch then!" Tezzy shouted with no compassion.

Chapter 25

After making sure Man-Man's shipment made it to Indianapolis, Music made his way toward Desiree and Amayo's office of law.

Attorney Desiree stood in the center of her ample office. She was dressed in none other than perfection. Her Alexandre Vauthier pant suit was tapered to perfection.

"Mrs. Desiree, you have a Music down here waiting to see you. He says he doesn't have an appointment, but he thinks you'll want to see him," Desiree's secretary said into the intercom.

"Send him up, please," Desiree said.

She slid on her pumps just as the door was being pushed open. Music stepped into the office with a duffle bag in hand. Desiree stared at him and then at the bag nonchalantly.

"How you doing?" Music asked, taking a seat without invitation.

"Make this short and brief, please," Desiree said with a warm smile on her face.

"So, I know you are working on my mans Uno's case, and I know you don't know me, but I have information that can and will help him out."

Desiree stared at him with a cocky look on her face. "Who says I need any help? Because my name speaks loud in the courtrooms," she says.

"This the deal. I'm not here to disrespect you or anything, but this is deeper than you think. The judge that has bro's case hates Blacks, and my boss, Jimmy, has his hands all in the case. I'm 100 percent sure that they'll be going to prison for life if you don't play your cards right. Even the prosecutor on the case is dating Jimmy's little cousin, and they had dinner last week. Money talks, and bullshit walks a mile. Here's $200,000 for Uno, and it's pictures in there of the judge, prosecutor, and my boss snorting drugs, so that will help you win your case," Music said, getting up and walking out the door.

***

Desiree sat across from Uno. She felt a sense of desperation coming from him. She knew he was a strong man, but it pained her to see another black man caged behind bars.

"Put a smile on your face. If I don't get you home, then my name isn't Desiree," she said, looking at Uno.

Uno released the stress from his body and smirked. "So, what are we up against?" Uno asked.

"Well, some dude dropped into my office the other day and gave me $200,000 and some pictures. He said his boss's name is Jimmy, and the plan is to get you life in prison."

Uno looked at her with his mouth open. "They, who?" he asked.

"The judge and the prosecutor are working with Jimmy to send you and LR up the river, but Music gave me these pictures that can help us out. The only thing we need is to make sure the snitch retracts his original statement, which implicates you and LR," Desiree said, laying the pictures on the table. "We don't need anything poppin' up."

Uno nodded in agreement. "Totally."

"You need to get a lead on the snitch," she said.

***

Nasty had everyone at the round table so that when Uno and LR called, they all could speak.

"As y'all know, bro and LR will be going to trial soon, so we all going to have to get our heads back in the game. Having money has relaxed us so much that we not focused anymore, but hold y'all thoughts," Nasty said.

"Bro, you there?" Nasty asked Uno.

"Yeah, what's hood?" He answered.

"Hold on," Nasty said, clicking LR in too.

"Now we all here at the round table," Nasty said, setting the phones in the middle of the table.

"Okay, this the deal, family. The nigga Fat D need to be found and taken care of before we go to trial. He's the only thing the feds have on us. The other person is Mix Breed, which y'all can leave alone. I know we haven't been having a good flow since we got knocked, but I promise, things will be back sweet soon."

Chapter 26

Crowds of people stood huddled in packs in front of Heaven's Funeral home on 24th MLK out west. 'R.I.H., Lipz' was plastered on the front of everyone's T-shirts.

Tears covered the majority of people's faces, while rage covered others. All in all, Lipz would definitely be missed. Being that she was the only female in their bunch, everyone looked at her like a sister, cousin, or just homie. The crazy thing about her was that she could chill with them like she was one of the niggas. She went on missions, fucked females with them, and busted her gun with the crew, so that alone made them respect her even more.

Man-Man, Two-Tall, Leo, and Coffee sat in the limousines parked at the curb in front of the funeral home. Every last one of them had a bottle in their hands. Two-Tall was taking it the hardest. His drinking was how he'd been keeping his sanity through the situation. Any other crew would have chalked it up to the game they were playing in. They all felt bad because they should have made sure she was always good. There would definitely be repercussions.

"Leave y'all guns in the car," Man-Man instructed them before stepping outside the limousine.

"My heat is part of my outfit, and I don't go nowhere without it," Leo said.

"Listen. I know this is hard for us all, but I promised Lipz's mother we would respect her wishes. I love Lipz. She was a big part of this crew, but her people don't want any weapons in the funeral," Man-Man said before turning around and giving Asap some love.

Man-Man, Two-Tall, Leo, Coffee, and Asap slowly walked down the aisle. The closer Two-Tall got to Lipz's casket, the more heat came off his body. Standing in front of her, he reached down and touched her face, which was as cold as ice.

"We will always love you, sis. Always. Then all five took their seats behind Lipz's mother.

Just as the choir finished singing, the doors to the funeral home opened. Gasps rang out throughout the funeral home as all eyes focused on the man who entered. Asap frowned at their blatant disrespect toward Lipz's family. Two-Tall's temper immediately flared.

"Fuck!" Man-Man whispered to himself about making everyone leave their pistols in the car. He had underestimated the situation. Everyone sat silent as they waited to see how things would play out. It was no secret to the streets that the Westside family was responsible for Lipz's death.

Lipz's mother was in an uproar as she sat back and watched Nasty open a bottle of Ace of Spades and turn it upside down on top of Lipz's body. Then he kicked the casket over, making Lipz's body roll out. Suddenly, Tezzy and Lil' E opened their coats, letting their Drakos echo throughout the funeral home.

Tat, tat, tat, tat, tat, tat!

Everyone started screaming and ducking low.

"This ain't a game!" Nasty hollered while walking toward the front to his waiting car.

The West Side family had sent a clear message. They were out for blood, and they were back to their old selves.

Chapter 27

It was a Thursday night, and Club Exotic in Anderson was extremely packed as usual. Women filled the place, but men still outnumbered them two to one. Huddles of small packs filled the bar. One particular table stuck out the most because of the bottles of Champagne that occupied the area. The group consisted of five men and eight women. The women sipped on Champagne, while the men gulped away on Remy and Goose.

"Bring us another bottle of Remy and Goose!" the man shouted to the waitress behind the bar. "And bring the check with that, too! I'm about to get out of here. I gotta get in the house!" he shouted with a smile. Right then, he was as drunk as could be, and it showed by the sweat that was dripping down his face.

The waitress came over, setting the bottles on the table. He then grabbed the check from her hand. "$4,500! Damn!" he shouted while digging deep in his Polo pants. He peeled $1,000 from his stack and handed it to the waitress.

"Keep the change, baby!" he said loudly, in a cocky manner. For the past year and a half, he'd been a regular there. He was one of the reasons females around the city came there every week. His name had been ringing bells throughout the town, and everyone loved him. The town called him Nap or Indianapolis.

"I'm out," he said, standing up, rocking back and forth.

"Let me help you out," one female said, helping him gain his balance.

"Damn," he slurred. "I'm fucked up all the way." He laughed. Everybody at the table laughed as well.

The female helped him take baby steps, but they had to stop in order for him to regain enough balance to take a few more steps.

It took them all of five minutes to make it through the club to the front door. She continued to help him slowly down the street, stopping at the corner where he was still rocking back and forth. He stood there, looking at the female and then at his BMW. He dug inside his pockets and handed the female the keys because he knew he was too drunk to even drive himself.

"I have to take a piss," he said, standing next to his car door. While he took a piss, the female stood behind him.

"You know, the whole time we were in the club, I just asked myself, is this nigga really up in here acting like he's the king of this town? Which he might be, since he ran from Indianapolis because he got Uno and LR locked the fuck up," the female said.

Hearing Uno and LR's names sobered him all the way up. He tried to turn his head but stopped when he felt the gun at the back of his skull.

"You already know what it is," she said as she used her other hand to dig inside the man's pockets. She grabbed the money and put it inside her bag. The man tried to turn around again to see who it was.

Boom! The .357 rang out.

The slug ripped into the back of the man's head.

Boom! Boom! Boom!

She let off three more into the man's body. Before trotting off to the car, she threw an Uno playing card on top of his body. She hopped in, and Nasty peeled off casually.

As soon as Nasty got the lead on Fat D, he didn't trust anyone else to do the job but himself or Brezzy. But that was out of the way. It was time to get his brothers home.

***

A week later...

The courtroom was packed with angry loved ones of the people they said Uno or LR had made disappear or killed. They were all there to witness justice be served against the murderers.

Uno smiled at the prosecutor to let him know he wasn't worried about anything as he and LR sat at the table, looking like they were on their way to a GQ photoshoot. Uno continued to scan the courtroom, and his eyes landed on Jimmy sitting in the back, who, in return, slid his thumb across his neck with a smile, letting Uno know he was done for. Uno just winked at him and turned back around.

Nasty, Tezzy, Breezy, and Lil' E sat in the row behind them for support. All four of their stomachs were making flips as they realized that this could be their last time seeing their brothers.

"We good. We will be home soon, watching this replay on MSNBC while getting some pussy," Uno said into LR's ear while smiling.

"Nigga, how you so sure about that when they about to put our whole life on the table?" LR asked, holding his gut as it bubbled.

"Your Honor, before we begin, we have evidence that the key witness was killed two weeks ago under the feds' watch, so there's no evidence linking the two defendants to any of the charges, and if we may, can we approach the bench?" Desiree asked.

"Yes," the judge said, showing the hatred he had for the two lawyers.

Desiree, Amaya, and the prosecutor walked to the front of the court.

"Your Honor and prosecutor, before we begin, I would like to show you these," Desiree said, laying a few pictures on the judge's desk.

As soon as they saw the photos, their faces turned red. The judge looked over at a smiling Uno.

"We will take a fifteen-minute break," the judge said, hitting his gavel and running out of the courtroom.

Inside the judge's office…

"How did you get your hands on these?" the judge asked as soon as his office door shut behind the prosecutor.

"That's neither here nor there. Now, this is the outcome. We already know both of y'all are dealing with Jimmy, but the big question is, are y'all willing to save y'all selves and the lifestyle or save Jimmy?" Desiree asked.

"We already put duffle bags in y'all's cars that contain $100,000 apiece, and we will give y'all all the pictures we have," Amay said, sitting in a chair.

"Okay, Jimmy has it out for them two. One reason is that Uno had sex with Jimmy's wife, and she had a son, and the second reason is that Jimmy felt that Uno and LR robbed him a while back. Jimmy also kidnapped Uno's woman, and he's been having her for the longest. To get y'all hands on Jimmy, they would have to get him over here in the states because, over in Mexico, he's the man with a lot of connections, but here's the information y'all need," the prosecutor said without thinking

Back in the courtroom…

"All, rise!" the bailiff called out as the judge entered the courtroom.

After taking his seat, he motioned for everyone to take their seats.

"Your Honor, in light of the new evidence, the state of Indiana requests an acquittal. We respectfully ask the court to dismiss all charges and that the defendants be released without prejudice," the prosecutor said, knowing he was blowing the biggest case of his career.

The whole courtroom went into an uproar.

The judge hit his gavel. "Order!" The judge looked at Uno and LR. "The courts find you two not guilty, and once you two are processed, you will be free."

Nasty, Tezzy, Lil' E, and Brezzy threw their hands in the air.

"Yes!" They all smiled. The bailiff escorted the two out of the courtroom.

"In breaking news today, federal investigators report that Mr. Brandon, aka Uno, and Mr. Brew, aka LR, were found not guilty. According to the investigators, the two ran 80 percent of the illegal activity coming and going through the Midwest. If anything went down in Indianapolis, they had their hands in it. The kingpins were brought down by one of their own friends, who turned informant after being arrested for serving as an undercover cop. He was their key witness but ended up getting killed when coming out of a nightclub in Anderson two weeks ago. Reporting live from downtown, it's Korean Black. Back to you in the studio, Mark!"

Chapter 28

Uno sat back on his bunk and dialed a number on the phone as he kept his eyes on the range to make sure no police crept up on him. As soon as the judge told him he would hit the streets, he paid a CO to bring him a phone so he could put a few moves together.

"Hello!" the man shouted with an agitated tone.

"Detroit Love?" Uno asked.

"Uh, who this be?"

"Is this Detroit Love or not?" Uno asked with uncertainty.

"Yes, who this?" he asked.

"Uno," he replied sternly.

"Uno? Who?"

"Indianapolis Uno, motherfucker! Stop playing like you know more than one Uno."

Detroit Love recognized who was on the other end. "What's up, bro!" he shouted with joy. "Long time, no hear from you. Where you been? Why haven't I seen you in almost two years?" he asked.

"I been locked down for some time, but soon, I will be at you," Uno claimed.

"So, things are good?"

"Can't be better," Uno said with confidence. You remember back in the days, you use to always say you was going to end up with that cash, but we never thought it would be selling diamonds?"

"Yeah, them was the days," Detroit Love said, smiling.

"I need something special done for my team. You already know how I get down," Uno said.

"Something special, like what? You have anything in mind?"

"Nah, I really don't know. I've been gone for almost two years, so a lot has changed. I don't know what's hot out there. I had a few small WSF chains. I need some extra big WSF chains for the big boys on the team, but they have to include watches, bracelets, and rings—the whole nine bro. We can't half do shit, feel me," Uno said.

"You know I take care of you. Let me hit a few numbers. Listen, for the big pieces, I need $225,000 and will charge you another $100,000 for fifteen small ones," Detroit Love said.

"Deal!" Uno said. "Make sure you put green stones in them. I need this done ASAP. I will have my people send you the money now."

***

Two-Tall was still furious about what occurred at Lipz's funeral, as he and the rest of the crew had been lying low, plotting their next move. They all had just finished watching the breaking news.

Tired of sitting up in the house, Two-Tall pulled a bag of guns from the small safe that sat behind a picture in his room. No one, not even Man-Man, knew of the guns he had stashed around their house.

Two-Tall, Asap, Man-Man, and Head all strapped on their vests. Asap held a blank expression on his face the whole time. He waited to make sure everyone was together before heading toward the front door. They all piled into Asap's BMW and sped off. Everyone sat quietly in their own thoughts as they maneuvered through the streets, heading toward The Land. Asap drove down 25th street, coming from

Haughville, and parked on the corner, next to Kim's Candy store.

"Get in the driver's seat and wait right here," Asap said, looking over at Two-Tall and then the crowd of dudes standing around the front of the store. Walking from the side of the building, Asap held up his AR and stopped the six WSF niggas conversation with bullets. They knew these niggas were on the low end of the West Side family, but they didn't care, because it all counted in the game called war.

Chapter 29

Man-Man and Two-Tall had put their little crew together and had the Southside going crazy with the dope they'd gotten from Jimmy. Fiends traveled all over the city so that they could get their hands on it.

In all, the crew included Man-Man, Two-Tall, Asap, Leo, Coffee, and Head. Leo already had a crew of his own that he planned on talking to about joining. For the time being, they were trying to get their money up because the disrespect the West Side family showed toward Lipz and her loved ones had to be handled one way or another.

Man-Man still felt some type of way about LR for the way he knocked him out a while back. He never got over his teeth getting knocked out, either.

Leo opened the door to let his guys in. After shutting and locking the door, they all took their seats.

"Listen, these are my little brothers. They have rode with me through a lot," Leo said. "Now, this is my man, Snow."

"What's good, y'all? I want y'all to know I'm here and down for whatever. My brother told me he needed me to get down with y'all movement, so I'm here," Snow said, giving everyone some dap.

"Next, this is Smash," Leo said, pointing toward a brown-skinned kid.

"I will always ride for my nigga. We grew up together and played in the same sandbox. They don't call me Smash for nothing," he said, smiling.

Leo grabbed $40,000 out of a bag and handed twenty apiece to Snow and Smash.

"What's this for?" Smash asked.

"This is for y'all to get right. We going to be dealing with y'all. We know y'all have a few youngstas under y'all, so we got some work we need y'all to put out there. We all going to get a cut. We giving y'all the twenty so y'all can pay y'all own crew. Here's a kilo of heroin, and we getting these for $45,000, so y'all price will be $55,000. It's a lot different than the cocaine y'all be pushing. Trust me," Leo said.

"This shit sound too good," Snow said, rubbing his waves.

"Listen. It's one thousand bricks in a kilo of heroin, so y'all sell each brick to the hustlers for $225, but if you do consignment, you hit them for $275 a brick. So off 150 bricks, you should be counting at $30,000," Leo said, smiling.

Man-Man, Two-Tall, and Head watched Leo school his brothers on the new game.

"Before y'all go, remember, a man who lives for himself is a failure. But the man who lives for others has achieved true success. It's not fair to ask of others what you are unwilling to do yourself. With that said, we will ride just as hard for y'all," Two-Tall said.

***

After Uno and LR signed their names on a few documents, they were on their way to the fresh air. As they both approached the last door, they smiled so big you could see all of their teeth. They couldn't believe that after eighteen months, their freedom was only a few feet away from them. They both thought their lives were over with.

They owed all the thanks to Music and their lawyers. They both walked through the door, stopping as they stared at each other and inhaled a deep breath of Indianapolis's street air.

A dark-tinted Infiniti truck pulled smoothly up to the curb. Uno paid close attention to the car and saw it had California commercial license plates. The passenger and the back passenger doors opened.

"Get in, niggas."

They both heard a voice they knew too well.

At the entrance, the pungent odor of Granddaddy Kush snatched their breath away. Ant blew rings into the air with a smile on his face.

"Welcome home," he whispered as he shook their hands.

Uno was so happy to see his brother that he damn near jumped into his arms.

"The world counted y'all out, but I knew y'all were coming back to the streets," Ant said.

"You know they can't hold us," LR said, smiling.

"Since we have y'all back out here, we have to keep y'all out here," Ant said with a solemn look on his face.

Uno looked over at him for a second before replying. "Let me worry about keeping myself out."

"Are y'all worried at all after beating the Feds?" Ant asked sarcastically.

"I'm not worried. Why would I be? Are you?" Uno asked, looking back at LR.

"Why would I be?" LR asked the same thing.

"Why would y'all be? Good questions. Y'all just did eighteen months locked up and almost was doing the rest of y'all life. Then y'all made the feds look like fools," Ant said.

"What are you saying, bro? Y'all don't think it's over?" Uno asked. "Listen. Legends don't retire. They reinvent, and with that said, we plan on taking back what's ours. We have jobs to do out here, and that pumps life back into these streets. Been sitting on the bench for eighteen months now, and these streets have took a turn for the worst since we been gone, but we're back, and it's nothing anyone can say or do to change that," Uno said.

"What you have to say, LR?" Ant asked.

"I'm willing to ride it out with bro," he said.

Ant was at a loss for words. All he could do was shrug his shoulders.

Chapter 30

Uno grabbed Brezzy by the hand and dragged her away. Cameras flashed, brightening up the extremely dark block. He dragged her up the stairs of Club Ruthie.

"This way, sir," the bouncer said as he led them across the thick, black carpet that extended from the top of the steps, down to the curbside.

As they entered the building, he peered from side to side cautiously. The sound of clapping and cheering echoed throughout the place. The sound of the music faded away, and the loud noise of the crowd increased.

"Welcome home!" the crowd screamed simultaneously. Uno's smile brightened up the room as he accepted the love. His heart was touched by the many banners that spread across the building. Nasty even had the waitresses wearing T-shirts that said "Welcome Home!"

"Uno and LR, come make a toast. Come on!" the deejay demanded.

They felt like they owed the city a toast, especially since they'd all come out to welcome them home. They dapped hands throughout the crowd, which was parting like the Red Sea as they strutted through it. The women looked at both men with desperation in their eyes as they pulled and tugged them. When they made it to the stage, microphones were handed to them. The place got quiet as everyone waited to hear from the two bosses.

Uno cleared his throat. "Look, y'all, I'm not going to take too much of y'all time, but I want to thank you all for coming out to party with me and LR. It's time to turn the heat all the way up. If you with us, then, love. If not, damn," Uno said.

The crowd went into an uproar, cheering away. After the cheering died down, LR spoke. "I told y'all once before we went in, we was coming back out here. We just made the whole world into believers once again. We back. Turn that shit up," LR said, walking away.

Uno and LR took a seat at the table where the family was sitting. As soon as Uno took his seat, Brezzy was all over him. He felt so grateful to have had the family in his corner. They did the entire eighteen months with them.

"We love y'all!" Uno yelled.

"We all love y'all, too!" Nasty yelled back.

Uno looked up and was surprised to find a small crowd had gathered around their table. He gave out hugs and love.

Later that night ...

Breezy was looking amazing all night and smelled even better. Uno scooted closer to her on the sofa and lifted her feet onto his lap.

"Take these heels off, and relax," Uno said as he helped her take them off. He began rubbing her feet while she looked over the rim of her champagne glass at him.

The look she was giving him made his dick rock straight up. As she noticed, she slid her right foot down to his dick. Not being able to withstand the tease, Uno pulled Brezzy toward him. With their faces inches apart and their hearts racing with lust in their eyes, Uno leaned in and kissed her lips. She tasted just as he imagined, like heaven. He slid his hand down the side of her face and then her arms.

While still kissing, he lifted her halter top over her head, revealing her perfect 32 D's with light nipples that were standing at attention. She tilted her head back and let out a deep sigh of satisfaction as Uno inhaled one of her breasts. He licked both of them until he felt the heat coming off her body. He unfastened the button on her skinny jeans and helped her peel out of them. She wasn't wearing any panties.

He sat back for a minute, trying to savor the moment and take in all her beauty, so he stood her up and spun her around in front of him. She was blushing from ear to ear as he admired her small body.

Uno's dick felt like it was going to bust at any moment. He quickly got undressed, then sat back down on the sofa. He pulled her to him and lifted her up, helping her mount the head of his dick.

"Oh…." Brezzy sighed as she slowly slid her tight pussy down. She arched her back, giving it that C shape, and gripped his dick like a seasoned vet, working her pussy muscles and throwing that soft, yellow ass down against his pelvis. He reached around and palmed both ass cheeks to help guide her up and down, but she reached back and slapped his hands off. She wanted to be in control, and he wasn't going to complain.

"Uno." She moaned as he kissed across her chest.

"Yeah," he whispered, voice a little quivered, and felt the pressure building up in his dick.

"I'm cumming," Brezzy said

Uno felt her walls contracting. She jerked violently, then continued throwing that ass on him while screaming, "Ah! Ah! Oh my God!"

Uno's stomach did back flips as his dick exploded. "Ah…" He groaned from the sensation. "I have never busted a nut like that before," Uno said, out of breath. Breezy leaned forward, resting her head on his chest with his half-limp dick still inside her. She began kissing him softly, getting him rock hard again.

Chapter 31

Nasty rode through the south side of the city and thought about how all his spots out there were coming up short. It wasn't like fiends stopped smoking. He had Tezzy and Lil' E on the phone.

"This shit crazy. One of the fiends gave me a folded-up paper that had heroin in it, and they calling it Red Bull," Nasty said.

"Yeah, bro, someone cutting throat," Lil' E said, blowing smoke out of his car window.

Nasty jumped on the highway, heading toward his hood. Not even a few minutes later, he was pushing his Porsche 911 Carrera 5/45 down Edgemont, the street he'd grown up on. Since it was mid-May, the hood was crowded with people. Parking, he checked his gun. Da land was known throughout the city for its money getters and ruthless killers. He grew up in the same trenches and was even part of the reason for their infamous reputation. He was born to go and stayed aware of everything going on around him. Tucking his heat, he exited the truck.

As he approached the modest brownstone house that sat in the middle of the block, all eyes were glued on him because it wasn't every day that they saw him pull up on the block.

"What's up?" Nasty greeted Boo, one of the hustlers from the block. Nasty looked Boo up and down and just smiled. He was looking at the epitome of the next generation's hustlers. Fresh Jordans laced his feet, complementing the crisp Pelle-Pelle outfit he wore that looked like it just came straight off the mannequin, snap back on his head, and a gold chain with the WSF logo on it hung from his neck, completing his ensemble perfectly.

Uno had the chains shipped to one of Nasty's stores, which gave them out to the ones who were worth wearing them.

Boo was only eighteen years old with a few bodies under his name. He was always ready to bust his gun for the cause, which was why he was perfect for Nasty's favorite block.

"Ain't shit been up around here, Big Homie. Same stuff," Boo stated. "But can I get a little of your time?" he asked, looking up and down the block.

"You know you can. What's up?" Nasty asked.

"Well, my cousin be messing with a dude named Snow, and he was pillow talking to her about some niggas that been taking over the Southside. With me knowing we have spots all over the city, I pushed her for more information, and it's that nigga Man-Man. They said he be moving out of Wood Workers Projects," Boo said.

"Good looking out, little homie," Nasty said.

***

Since the night of the welcome home party, Uno had been spending his time getting used to being back on the streets. He'd basically been home, spending time with Brezzy and his daughter, just enjoying his freedom. Since he gave them most of his time, he felt like it was time to get reacquainted with the streets. He was so out of touch, and he knew his crew had let the money blind them, so he called his little homie Reese to come through and help him get caught back up on things. He didn't want to be in the spotlight; for that moment, he would play the background.

Uno sat behind the steering wheel of a black Lexus. While the passenger talked, he looked at the clear, blue sky.

"This right here is another money block out this way. With the right dope, it can do numbers," the young dude said.

Uno knew the passenger as King, but he'd been away for years, so Uno had to get used to him again. For the moment, King would help him out by being his ears and eyes on the streets. Reese put them back in touch when Uno called him.

Reese was in California, where he caught a case, and the feds gave him twenty-five years, but thanks to Uno and Nasty, he had one of the best lawyers working on his appeals. Even while incarcerated, Reese controlled a great portion of the crew. BTG had come a long way from having only four members to about twenty. Reese gave the command to work hand in hand with Uno and make sure he had everything he needed.

Uno rode through the city, mad. The condition of the city was bad. The entire city looked like a ghost town. Before he got locked up, there was money to be made out on the blocks. He understood why Nasty fell back, but he didn't understand Lil' E and Tezzy.

"Slow down. Right here," King instructed. "See, this is the new Wood Works," he said as he pointed to some newly built apartments. "Lotta money out here, too. They get it on when it's dope out here. Look at all the dope fiends coming and going out of there. Man-Man and his crew be in there, though," King said.

"Man-Man?" Uno asked with confusion. "Man-Man buys from you?" Uno asked with his mind spinning.

"Yeah, he used to, but now he got some dope called Red Bull, so he been doing his thing out here with the crew," King said.

"I'm going to adapt to the times. Follow my lead, and we gon' make a lot of bread. I listened to you for over two hours, tell me about different spots. When I was out here, it was only my crew, but I'm going to make sure they turn on the lights in this city again. We all about to eat," Uno said.

"How much money have you had in your life?" Uno asked.

"No more than $25,000 all at once, and that was when you gave us the spot years ago," King said.

"Well, I'm going to show you what life is really about. You heard," Uno said.

"I hear you," he replied with hunger in his eyes. "All you got to do is tell me where to start, and I will round up the crew and ride," King said, meaning every word.

"Well, if they not with us, they against us. That's where you start," Uno said, pulling up to a block.

"Enough said, bro. Say no more," King said and got out of the car.

Uno pulled off, thinking about all the money he was about to make.

Chapter 32

The next day…

King stood in front of about twenty young TTG (Trained to Go) members. His demeanor was laid back, but his words were full of aggression. Being back in the city gave him a full charge, and he got word from Reese that Uno was back, so that only meant he was as well.

"From here on out, everything goes through us! Whoever isn't screaming TTG or WSF, then they against us! We want in on everything from dope to pills being sold in the city. There will not be any more freelancing around here. We back, and we about to eat from every plate. We all about to get money, so there's no way any of you should be broke again. We taking everything over. Time is money, so let's get it cracking and get everyone that's not with us out the way so the road can be filled with us. I'm hungry," he said, rubbing his stomach. "Y'all hungry, right?"

They all replied, "Hell yeah!"

"Well, let's get it then! We gon' go through this city. Leave no one standing."

Meanwhile…

The black charger sat in the parking lot of Desiree's and Amayo's law office.

"Okay, just as we figured he would," Agent Peck spoke. "Knew he would be coming to visit the two sooner or later," he said as he took pictures of Uno getting out of a Lexus. The agent took a few more shots before Uno walked into the office.

Agent Grant sat in the passenger seat, watching Uno. He came into the case in the middle, and every time he saw a picture of Uno and LR, it sent chills up his spine. Throughout his time as an agent, he never dealt with anyone like the two. He had heard so many stories about the two crime bosses. He knew his boss had a hard-on for the two since they made the feds look crazy by beating their case, but he wished he could give the case back.

Uno st before the distraught-looking Desire. On the table in front of them lay a few pictures. Desiree looked at Uno and put her head down.

"I don't know how to tell you, but look at them," she said, handing him the stack of pictures from her desk.

Uno grabbed them and flicked through them. Sweat beads started to form on his face as he flicked picture by picture.

"Who?" was all he could get out.

"We have a business relationship, but I look at you like we are family now, so promise me you won't do anything stupid," she said.

"Stupid? I never do anything like that," he said with sarcasm. Uno stared into Desiree's eyes with no emotion whatsoever. He didn't say a word.

"Promise me you'll get yourself together first, bro."

"Can't promise you anything, but I'm going to paint the city with blood until I get all the info I need to get her back home," he said, getting up and rushing out of the office, calling LR and Nasty.

Uno made it in time to see Nasty pull up to LR's crib. Nasty could see the hurt in Uno's eyes, so he knew whatever it was, it was deep in his chest. LR opened the door as soon as they stepped in front of it. He also knew something was up by the sound of Uno's voice.

LR and Nasty watched as Uno paced the room in a distraught manner. He faced them with tears in his eyes.

"They have her. She been with this nigga the whole time. I feel like I gave up on her, man," Uno said, laying the pictures on the table.

Neither of them was ready for what they saw. LR's body started shaking as he looked at them. A million thoughts ran through their minds.

"Bro, we have to get her back," LR said.

"I know, but we have to think smart. I know that nigga Man-Man is fucking with that nigga Jimmy, so we have to get our hands on him and get all the info we can get," Uno said.

Chapter 33

Man-Man had Snow and Smash sitting outside of one of the West Side family trap houses. Hopping out, they walked up the driveway to the front door, which was open behind the screen, knowing they both waited.

"Yo, who the fuck knocking on the door like that?" Tezzy asked, getting up from between a female's legs.

No matter how much money the two made, they still loved to be in the middle of the action every day. Tezzy walked up to the screen with his shirt off and a gun on his hip.

"Who the fuck—" Tezzy started to say before two gunshots rang out, hitting him in the chest.

Lil' E jumped out of the chair, snatching his .40 caliber from his hip. He let off rounds, making the two dudes back away. He ducked as bullets riddled inside of the house. He ran toward the door with the .40 caliber, shooting through the screen, catching one of them in the back as they were hopping in their car.

"Bro, you good?" Lil' E asked.

"No. It hurt," Tezzy said, closing his eyes.

Lil' E dialed 911 on his phone, and he called Uno, LR, and Nasty afterward.

"Bro, we need ya help," Lil' E said.

"What's good?" Uno asked, feeling something was wrong.

"We on 26th, and we been hit!" Lil' E said.

It was good that they were all riding together, checking out the hood. Nasty hit a few buttons, and his stash spot popped out. Uno grabbed his MP5, Nasty grabbed the .40 caliber, and LR grabbed his .357.

"We ain't been home a whole month, and all this bullshit already?" At the same time that they were rolling a stretcher out the cut, Uno and them were pulling up to the block.

An old lady, named Sister, from the block stopped Uno. "There was a shooting in the house, and they took the little light one on the stretcher and the other one out before the police came."

Later that night…

Four masked men stood in the back of the house in Haughville. Each of their hands gripped semi-automatic pistols. Two of them stood on both sides of the door, while the other two stood in front of the door. They'd just sent their runner inside to get a bag of hydro. One of the men's phones vibrated. He looked down and saw a text saying he was coming out.

"Game time," he said to his accomplices. They gripped their guns tightly and prepared for the work.

In seconds, the door opened, and a man stepped out. The two gunmen on the side rushed the house violently with their guns waving back and forth. One of the men who stood in front of the door grabbed a dude who tried rushing out of the door. He shoved the man inside before him.

"Everybody, lay the fuck down!"

All the men inside froze in their positions, staring. Mounds of money were stacked in front of each of them.

"Drop all that money in y'all hand, and lay the fuck down!" the gunman said as he shoved the man onto the floor. The other three went around, throwing all the other men to the floor, with crazy looks in their eyes.

Once everyone was lying on their stomachs, the man shouted, "You move, you dead! But you all have one chance to put all y'all pistols in front of y'all because if we have to shake y'all down, then I'm going to blow your wig back!"

In seconds, roughly ten pistols sat in a pile on the floor. One of the gunmen grabbed a bag out of the trash can and put all the guns inside. He threw the bag to one of the gunmen who stood at the back door and started going through everybody's pockets. He put money, wallets, jewelry, and phones in a separate bag. He then made his way around the room, piling the money from the floor in the same bag. When he was all done, he looked over at the gunman at the door and gave him a nod.

The gunman who stood at the door walked over to the men who were lying on the floor, scared. They were so scared that they were stiff. A gunman snatched a man from the middle with dreads and made him get on his knees. The man, frightened, looked up at the gunman.

"Come on, please," he pleaded.

"Please, what, muthafucka? You fuck with Man-Man, right?" he asked as he placed the gun against the man's forehead.

"Yeah, but that's just to get some money," the man they called Head said

The gunman squeezed the trigger quickly. *Boc!* The victim's brains flew all over the other men on the floor. Then the gunman aimed at Head's body and fired. *Boc! Boc! Boc! Boc!* All the other men watched, thinking they would be next. The gunman then looked at his accomplices.

"We out!" he shouted. In seconds, they were out of the house, making their getaway in the darkness.

The assignment was given by Nasty, Uno, and LR. It had nothing to do with their plans to take the city back. It was all personal, but they killed two birds with one stone. The murder victim had been in Man-Man's crew, and he was the one who sent the boys to Lil' E and Tezzy.

After doing their homework, Uno, Nasty, and LR found out he had always run an illegitimate gambling house at night. He made all his money from that spot. WSF had just begun, but was trying to get it over with before a war started because they had other things to handle.

Chapter 34

The next day...

Uno, LR, and Nasty hit the highway and ended up in ATL at a car dealership. Uno and LR hadn't been there before but had been doing business with them for years. On the other hand, Nasty had been there a few times. It was like a dream for Uno and LR.

As they all stood with their eyes fixed on the beautiful hunk of steel, Uno's dick got hard. While he was locked up, he always told himself, when he got home, he was going to get one. When he saw Ant pull up in the hood in one, he knew he had to have one.

"Damn." Uno sighed as he walked around the hunk. "I can't believe this," he said to himself as he stared at the all-white boy Rolls-Royce Phantom VII SUV.

LR stood off to the side, staring at another SUV. The SUV he was staring at was also a hunk of steel. It was a Bentley Bentayga.

"Holy shit! Is that Nasty?" a tall, black man shouted.

Uno, LR, and Nasty span around to the voice.

"What it do, baby?" Nasty asked, dapping the man up. "These are my brothers," Nasty said.

"I know who they are by watching the news," Puma said. "I'm happy y'all beat their ass," he said, talking about the feds

"What can I do for y'all, anyway? Tell me."

"You can start by giving my brothers the keys to that Rolls and Bentley, and I will take the keys to my baby," Nasty said.

"Hold on for a second," Puma said, rushing off.

Meanwhile in Indianapolis...

Lil' E and King crept up East Street out south in Lil' E's black Camaro. They watched a group of men standing in the middle of the block, having the time of their lives. Lil' E pulled up a few cars in front and parked. "Come on," he said as he led the way.

They walked confidently toward the men. The men watch with baffled looks on their faces. They all knew who Lil' E was, but had only seen King around, and they still stood there, watching them, wondering why they were on their block. They'd seen Lil' E ride by a few times, but that was his first time stopping. Their guts told them that some bullshit was about to go down because they knew the little war with the WSF and Man-Man's team was going on. Even though they weren't down with Man-Man, he's been plugging them with the dope.

"What's good?" Lil' E shouted as he stood in front of the group. No one said anything. They all stared back at him and King. "Damn, what's good?" He smiled. "Why y'all have that look on y'all face? I know y'all wondering what I'm doing on y'all's block since I never stopped before." He continued to smile as he waited for one to speak. "Y'all looking like y'all want to do something, but y'all thinking like … nah," he said. "I ain't on no bullshit. I'm here on other shit," Lil' E said.

"Why you on my block for then?" one man asked with a calm demeanor. The man was the leader of the group, and the streets called him Dollar. Dollar was what you called an old head. He'd been in the game since he was eleven years old. He was forty, so the group called him OG. He was a stand-up dude, and most of the dudes his age were dead, in jail, or cracked out. Dollar knew he had to shift with the times, so he had hand-picked a group of young niggas.

"Why are we here? It's crazy ya ask that because I know you been getting plugged by Man-Man, but we going to look past that. I just like how you run this block. It reminds me of back in the day. It's like your own little world out here." He smiled. "I just wanna bring y'all to the table," Lil' E said.

"To the table? What ya talking about? Because I have my own table," Dollar said with an agitated look.

"We bring everything to the table, and we all eat off the same plate. I'm coming at you first because I respect the movement you have going on, and I don't want to just say fuck you," Lil' E said.

"What?" Dollar laughed. "I'm good. I do me this way. I'm the boss over this way, and that shit ya spitting ain't on shit," he said, showing all his teeth.

"On the real, you know how the WSF get down, so stop playing yourself, and get down before you have to lay down," Lil' E said with fire behind each word.

Dollar waved him off like he was one of his females. "Aye, man, dig this. I ain't getting down and damn sure not laying down unless it's with a bitch or pile of money. Ask about me. Since your pops is home now, call him up and ask about Dollar. I'm a legend around this city and not you, Uno, Nasty, or LR ever going to be able to walk in my shoes," he said.

"Enough said… No more needed to be said," Lil' E said as he spun on his heels before spinning back around. Surprisingly, he's gripped a .40 caliber with a thirty-round clip. He aimed at Dollar's face.

Boc! Boc! Boc! Boc! Dollar's body fell onto its back with the head wide open. The group of men took flight. King was right behind them, letting loose. *Boc! Boc! Boc! Boc!* Boc! King hit everyone in the group.

Lil' E and King fled toward the car and pulled off.

Chapter 35

Man-Man sat inside his BMW in the back of his projects, rolling a blunt. He peeked up from the blunt every so often to see what was going on around him. Drug activity was pouring from everywhere. Every drug someone wanted could be bought out of there.

A jeep swerved wildly around him and parked. The small, lanky man got out and walked toward him. He snatched the passenger door open and got inside.

"What it do?" the man asked, watching how Man-Man's people surrounded the truck as soon as he got in. He reached over for a dap, and Man-Man returned it. He was a fellow WSF gang member who went by the name of Mix.

Man-Man kept his pistol on his lap. He felt that if he could trade on his team, then he would throw him to the curb at any time, so he didn't trust him or like him for that reason. Man-Man kept him close for the simple fact that he knew everything that went on in the city. He stayed in the mix of whatever, and that was how he got his name. Man-Man paid him to be his eyes and ears in the streets, and so far, it was helping him.

"So what's the deal?" Man-Man asked as he stared through Mix.

"Uno is back on the streets, and they been on that 'get down or lay down' shit. Niggas that been going against them been found dead where they stand. They even fucked up Dollar and his team," Mix said.

"I been wondering what happened to the old head, but that shit Uno and them on isn't going to fly this way," Man-Man said, hitting the blunt. "This what I want you to do. Put it out there that we looking for them," Man-Man said, handing Mix a wad of cash.

One hour later...

The Rolls-Royce, Bentley, and, bringing up the rear, another Rolls-Royce, entered the complex. All the drug activity and jokes ceased for a few seconds. Two of the men quickly took their places in front of Man-Man and Two-Tall, not knowing what was to come. A third man pulled his gun out but hid it behind his back. Man-Man and Two-Tall looked around to make sure all their men were on point, and they were all ready for war.

The trucks stopped directly in front of the huddle of men. The window rolled down on the first Rolls. Uno wanted them to see his face before he got out. He stepped out with fire in his eyes. Then Nasty and LR did the same. All three had bulletproof vests over their T-shirts.

"I heard someone is looking for us?" Uno asked, staring at all of them. "Y'all wanted us. We here. What's up?" he asked as he began to step closer to them.

Man-Man finally spoke. "You painting the perfect pictures!" Man-Man mocked. "They finally let y'all out, huh? Welcome home! I see y'all still at it," he said, pointing to the trucks. "They cute. The streets is watching y'all, so I wouldn't expect anything less, but don't trip. I'm going to give them something to really watch."

"As you should," Uno replied modestly. "If your paper up, then go for what you know."

"If my paper up? Shit has changed since the last time you were on the streets. What it's been? Two years? We getting real money out here!"

"One thing about money is anybody can get it, but what's money to you? Because by the looks of your men out here, you can't be doing too much," Uno said.

"I know what money is," Man-Man replied with a smile.

"I guess the streets haven't told you, me and my teams running shit on this side," he said.

"Nah, I haven't heard about that."

"Ask around." Man-Man smiled. "No team out here doing numbers like us."

"You know, just because you doing better than the next doesn't mean you up. It just mean you have one more dollar than them right now. Anyway, you should be rich right now since your team is the only one doing numbers, as you put it. You only as good as your competition," Uno said.

"Competition is nothing. Like I told you, my team is running shit now, so all that other shit ya have going on in the city, you need to stop while ya ahead," Man-Man said.

"I hear you, big dawg, but it seems to me like you bragging about running the city that looks bad. We come home, and the city looks like a ghost town. It's a bunch of muthafuckas starving out here, ready to eat, but don't trip, because we about to feed everyone. Don't worry. I got a spot for you and your team at the table, but it would be where my dogs eat. You going to feel our presence. We going to show you how to carry a whole city on your shoulders. We beat the feds; now they going to have to send the SEAL team for us this time. Better yet, save that little money you have because you know our get down because when we done, you might be able to get a few thousand. That bullshit ass dope you have is nothing. I'm about to show you. We still spending Red's and Jimmy's money, nigga. We haven't even touched the new money," Uno said, throwing a wad of old-face hundreds.

Uno was livid, but he was hiding it too well. He would never let them see that he was shitty. Uno hit the button, and the end of Rod Wave's "All I Got" came from the speakers.

"Your teeth look real good," LR said, hopping back into his truck.

Man-Man's crew never saw inside the trucks because of the tints, which had three more people in each of them.

Uno and them paid attention to the small group of men who stood by the exit in a small crowd. They appeared as if they weren't paying attention to the three trucks.

"Fuck it. Let's make this shit count since they want to be on the other side," Uno said as he hit the power window button. Let's take all in front of us," he said to the three dudes in the truck with him.

The sound of the Mac-11s and Uzis echoed through the whole hood. One man fell on his face as the others' heads split open. Two other men fled in different directions. As the three dudes in Uno's car took the two that were fleeing, Nasty's and LR's car were taking everything else.

Blocka! Blocka! Blocka! sounded off from an unfamiliar gun. They all looked around to see where the shots were coming from. The bullets bounced off the trucks.

Halfway down the block, they still heard gunshots.

"Everyone coo'?"

They all checked themselves as Uno zipped up the block. "All good," they all said with gratitude.

"I love this type of shit. War, it is," Uno said with a grin on his face. He turned up the Webbie song he had playing.

Chapter 36

Uno sat outside at the small table of Ant's Grill in Miami. To his right sat Nasty, Breezy, and LR, and to the left sat Ant and Lil' E. They all sat close so no one could hear what their conversation was about.

"Dig, this is how it's going down," Uno whispered. "I'm going to which over to the dope game. We been gone, so we going to move with the times. It's time to play ball. I know you don't want us to get out there, bro," he says, looking at Ant, "but I can't leave the city the way it is. Plus, we have to get our ends back up if we going to get her back," he said, handing Ant a stack of pictures.

Ant flipped through the pictures, shaking his head. "Damn," he said.

"This is what's first on the list. We got to get the nigga Man-Man out the way because we been playing games with him. I been fucking with these New York dudes on the dope, but it's not the best, so we have to find a plug that can hold us down," Nasty said.

"Well, I can help y'all with that," Ant said.

"Listen, at the rate we going, all of us would be locked up. We just beat the feds not even a month and a half ago, so we have to move more smoothly. Look at it like this. If the connect Ant is about to plug us with can't give us a ten, then we shouldn't be fucking with them. We are supposed to have the best dope. Lil' E and King have cleared the path for us," LR said.

Breezy just sat back, thinking about how she would break the news she'd just received to Uno.

"I'm a month past my period," she said, looking at Uno. Everybody just looked between the two. Uno's mouth hung wide open. "Say something, nigga," she said.

"What you want me to say? Because you already know how I feel about kids. I need all my babies," Uno said.

"Let's wrap this meeting up so they can talk amongst themselves," Nasty said.

"Okay. Any update on Tezzy or the niggas that did this to my little nigga?" Uno asked.

"Naw, he's still in a coma," Lil' E told them.

***

It took only a few hours to get from Miami to Houston, and that ride was what Uno needed. It gave him enough time to get all his thoughts right. He knew the feds were watching them, so they couldn't take any slip-ups, but he still knew the game had to go on. Ant pulled into the parking lot behind the small, run-down Mexican bar.

"Listen, after we get sis back, I'm out the picture. These dudes are fucked up, so, don't take it personal, but they don't deal with blacks. I know them because bro was fucking with them back in the day, and we always did good business. I still keep in touch with the little brother. He's a good dude. He's about that money. Big bro used to deal with the older brother. The little brother just came home from doing a five-year bid in the feds and took off like a rocket. If you had ridden that Rolls up here, they would have turned us back around. You see I had to pull this old, dirty jeep out," Ant said.

Minutes later ...

Uno walked behind Ant as he led the way toward the back of the bar. Ant knocked on the door three times, and it opened instantly. The small man who opened the door stared a hole through Uno. Uno felt the heat but kept his cool. He could tell that he was the older brother Ant was talking about in the car.

Ant looked over at Uno, who he knew was ready to say something. The younger-looking man who was sitting at the table, Gucci'd down, said something to the smaller man in Spanish, which got him to leave the room. The younger man stood up and walked toward them.

"My bad about my brother. He's having a bad day," he said as he got closer to them. He looked at Ant as if Uno wasn't in the room.

"Pedro, this is my little brother I was telling you about," Ant said. "He's a good dude."

"I don't know if Ant told you, but I just came home and am not ready to meet new people, but because of him, I can look past it. I take his word is bond. Plus, he says you his little brother, so I know y'all bloodline is good. I don't like long meetings, because time is money," Pedro said.

"As far as the long meetings go, I'm with you on that because time is money, and I have a whole city that's waiting. I don't want no handouts or any of that. Like I said, I have a whole city waiting on me, so all I need is a plug that can handle all this money I'm willing to bring to the table."

The man sat back with a smile on his face. "I might be the right person for you," Pedro said, leaning back in his chair.

"I damn sure hope so," Uno said.

"You know, I dig your swag. I been talking to you for the last ten minutes, and the whole time, you kept eye contact. I'm a good judge of character, and I listen to my gut. Where you from again?" Pedro asked.

"Indianapolis," Uno said with pride and with his chest poked out. "When my brother said I was his little brother, he wasn't lying. We came out the same pussy," Uno said.

"So Big Dawg—"

"Is my oldest brother," Uno said, cutting him off.

"Me and my brother got your brothers rich," he said with a grin on his face. "I'm sure you're familiar with all the dope they were getting. I been trying to get Ant to take some of it off my hands, but he's not going for it. I want to get the rest of this dope off my hands. I found some pounds of it the other day and hit my mans in Dallas, and he said it's an eleven. I have a silly recipe for it. The thing is, a few people dead off it, so I would add a little more of this and take a little of this, so my folks asked to turn it down to an eight because it brought too much attention to their city," he said.

"Okay, I want you to turn it all the way up, and if you can promise me every time, it's going to be the same, I want in," Uno said. "But I'm going to keep it one hundred. I'm not with this back and forth. It's not me to buy and get it back, so we have to move smarter. Feel me?" Uno said.

"Anything I give you is guaranteed to be top grade. Just ask your brother. Anytime they came through, it was the same. It will always be a ten, nothing lesser, so the back and forth is just a waste of time," Pedro said.

Uno smiled while nodding his head up and down. "Now, let's get this money."

Chapter 37

Smash drove the black jeep through the intersection of Post Road while the three passengers locked their eyes on the purple BMW that was pulling up to the pump slowly. Just as the vehicle stopped, the passenger hopped out and walked toward the store.

"Smash, lemme out right there!" Snow shouted from the backseat. Smash stopped short, just past the stone.

"Meet ya'll in the front!" Snow said, getting out.

"Let's go! Let's go!" Man-Man said.

Smash zipped through the entrance and pulled in front of the BMW.

"That's good!" Man-Man shouted. It was crazy that he could even speak at that point, being that he was so high off the K-Z blunt he'd just smoked to the head.

"Ready?" Two-Tall asked Man-Man as he tied the black bandana around his face. He then gripped the two .357s that he held in his hand.

Man-Man wrapped his mask around his face. "Yeah, let's go for it," he confirmed.

"Let's go!" Two-Tall said as he opened the door. Man-Man hopped out right after him.

Babyface looked up just in time to see the two masked men hopping out of the jeep. He attempted to go for his gun under his seat, but it was already too late.

Two-Tall began shooting first. *Boom! Boom! Boom!* The window shattered instantly.

Man-Man followed. *Boc! Boc! Boc!*

Two-Tall continued firing, hitting Babyface all in the chest. Cars began speeding out of the parking lot. Babyface's mans saw all the action from inside the store and decided to run out, blazing his gun.

Boc! Boc! Boc! He came out, firing. The man was so busy firing away that he didn't see Snow sneaking up from behind the store.

Boom! Boom! The man tumbled face-first onto the asphalt.

Days later...

King stood in the center of the courtyard, observing his surroundings. Packs of people swarmed throughout the projects. They'd been giving away dope all morning, so people were damn near tackling each other just to get to the dealers. They were scared that the dealers might run out of dope before they got their blaze.

King stood there, shaking his head, mad at the world, thinking about all the money he could have pocketed instead of giving out samples. They were going to buy anything anyway. The night before, Lil' E pulled up on him and gave him some bricks. He also gave strict instructions from Uno to give away every brick for free. Lil' E made King shake on it that he would give away the samples from 11 a.m. to 3 p.m.

Heroin addicts from all over the city had to come through to get their sample after hearing how good the dope was. The word spread near and far. The city of Indianapolis had never had any dope that good before.

King could tell the dope was a plus ten because he watched the bent-over addicts nodding off, looking like the walking dead, or their noses would start bleeding. In all the time he'd been in the game, he'd never seen anything like it before. That was the second time Uno had made him a believer. Uno's word had always been bond.

Minutes later...

A Rolls-Royce pulled into the parking lot. King looked hard as his crew stood on point. His phone rang. He looked down at the name, and the word "ONE" was spelled out. He answered with no hesitation.

"Yup," he whispered into the phone.

"That's me," Uno said before hanging up.

King started to walk hurriedly toward the truck. He lowered himself into the passenger seat, Uno leaning back, listening to a Boosie song. He was staring at the sight of the projects, and seeing money flowing everywhere took him back a little bit.

"No, this is what it's supposed to look like across the whole city. And by the time we done, it will be, so what's the read on it?" he asked King.

"They saying the city ain't never seen dope like this," he said.

"That's good, but I could tell at first, you was doubting me, but now I see your eyes are saying something else. Take care of them people out there because they the ones that's going to get you rich. Also, remember, if you take care of them, they'll take care of you in return. Give them jobs like keeping the projects clean, just small shit. Feel me?" Uno said. "This is only the beginning. I'm about to turn it up, lil' bro. Now that we know we have the best dope in the city, in a few days, you will have a few thousand bricks."

"King, you been part of my family since y'all was young. Yeah, y'all been gone for years, and I know you ain't never been in the game at this level, so just follow my lead. We doing each point for ten dollars," Uno said.

King sucked his teeth. 'That ain't gon' work, bro. They have five-dollar bags," he said.

"This dope going to sell itself. Plus, you just told me the word is that the city ain't never seen dope this good. We setting the price, and watch what it do," Uno said, looking at King.

150

"Bro, these muthafucka can barely get a five-dollar bag to get high off of."

"That's 'cause the dope is trash out here. Motivate the people out here, and I promise you, it will all come together. Plus, if I'm not mistaken, there shouldn't be no other team out here besides us, right?" Uno asked.

"Well, we still got to get at Man-Man, and Baby J is running Sutton Place," King said.

Uno turned his head so fast that he damn near snapped his neck out of place when he heard his cousin's name.

"Listen. Don't worry yourself about them. Just go on and get money," Uno said.

"Bro, it's hard times out here really. Niggas ain't got no money."

"We're going to give them something to compare to the bullshit dope out here. Motherfuckers is gon' be out of business. The only niggas who gon' be eating is the people at our table. We're going to raise the price, and that's going to push all these broke niggas to come to work for us. Fuck all that two-hundred-a-brick shit. You paying $185 a brick. You hit your team with it at $265; that's just fronting it to them. Now, if you want to wholesale, that's coo', too, because you hit them for $275, and everybody else outside of us pays $300," Uno broke it down for him.

"Bruh, you out here tripping. No nigga out here doing them numbers," King said, shaking his head.

"Listen to me. Either set shit up, or I will give the sack to one of them niggas out there, and I bet my last dollar they get money. You the only nigga in the city with this dope. You will have a few thousand in your hands in a day or so. We about to change the city," Uno said.

Chapter 38

The Rolls-Royce crept through Indianapolis International Airport. Uno was in search of his little brother. It didn't take him long to locate the man he was looking for. The little, black nigga wearing prison-issued clothes stood out like a sore thumb.

"There he go," Uno said, pointing at the man. Breezy drove the car over to the curb and parked. The man stood back and paid attention to everything that moved around him. The people coming and going from the airport knew the man was a threat, so that alone made them steer clear of him.

The man's name was Reese. He was the leader of TTG and had been locked down for a few years.

"Yo!" Uno shouted, catching the attention of everyone who stood on the curb.

Reese turned to see Uno waving his hand in the air. Reese rushed toward the car. Uno got out to greet him with a hug. Reese flashed a smile as he hugged him back.

As they pulled away from each other, Reese looked to see who was in the car with Uno. After seeing Brezzy, his smile faded off his face. Uno opened the back door for him to get in and slammed the door as he hopped in the front seat.

"What's good?" Uno asked with a bright smile.

"Shit, what can I say?" Reese replied, returning a smile of his own. "I'm home, without a dime to my name. It has to get better for me."

"Money isn't shit. You just get ready?" Uno said, handing Reese a small bag.

"You know I was born ready for whatever. Damn, bro. Thanks for the cash," Reese said.

"Well, let's get to it then," Uno said.

***

Uno, Nasty, and LR stood in the center of Sutton Place on the far east side. It was 8 a.m., and the projects were packed like it was a block party. People swarmed the courtyards like there was a parade going on. Addicts poured in from the entrance. They zipped in and out of the courts. Each corner was packed with addicts bent over with their noses buried in the packets of dope. Other addicts were huddled up, using each other's syringes.

All three, Uno, Nasty, and LR, had never seen anything like that in their lives. The crack era was something, but it was a whole new ball game. They really couldn't believe their eyes. Uno was just at King's spot, but it wasn't anything like that.

Uno looked over to his right, where a young teen boy stood with his back to the wall and a bag in his hand. In front of him was a line that consisted of about fifty customers.

"Here, Auntie. Take one. Let me know what it do," the boy said as he handed the woman a bag.

"Thank you, baby!" she shouted. "What's the name of it?"

"Walking Dead! It's fire! That's what we gon' have out here for a few hours so check us out!" the boy said.

They came up with the name late at night the previous night while discussing Man-Man. They needed everyone out of the way so they could get to the next thing on their list of business. That was one of the reasons they were out here to holler at Baby J.

They'd been watching the boys give away samples for two hours. Baby J ran the projects, and he'd been dealing with dope way before them. He promised them that nothing could touch what he was getting from his plug. He was moving almost twenty bricks per day of the dope he already had his hands on. There was no way he would cut off his connect to get dope of a lesser stature from Uno, just to make his cousin happy.

They had already given away about $5,000 worth of dope, which was nothing to them because they understood that the kickback would be incredible. They knew the product they had was the best. They were sure the customers who had been getting the free samples would only come back with more people.

"Uno, Nasty, and LR, come here!" Baby J said as he stood with a raggedy-looking woman.

"What's up?" They walked over to him.

"This is my main tester right here. She knows dope, and I trust her to keep it real with me at all times. I gave her a bag to see what it was. Mrs. Bow, how is it?" Baby J asked the old lady. Right at that moment, the old lady was in the middle of a big nod, where she was bent over, her head touching the ground.

"Mrs. Bow!" he shouted as he tapped the old lady to wake her up. "Wake up, damn! How is it? Keep it real, too," Baby J said.

"Anghh," she whined with her eyes shut. "Like I said. It's the best I ever had in my life, and I been doing this since the late eighties. It's too damn strong."

"What?" Uno asked, shocked at what he was hearing. He'd never heard an addict say some dope was too strong.

"Soon as I hit it, it rushed to my brain."

"How about the drain?" Baby J asked.

"The drain there, too. The drain came quick," she whined.

"What that mean? You don't like it?" Uno asked, completely baffled.

"I love it. Like I said, the drain there." She sniffed. "And the hit, too. If you ask me, you can cut it a little. Angghh... Trust me. I know dope, and this, what you have on your hands, is uncut heroin."

"What's better? This or that Baby World?" Baby J asked as he prepared himself for the answer.

"Baby World ain't got a shot next to this. Baby World is good, but this shit is better. I rate this a solid fifteen-plus," Mrs. Bow said, going into another big nod.

"Yeah?" Baby J asked, looking at Uno, Nasty, and LR with a slight smirk on his face.

"I told you, ain't nothing fucking with this," Uno gloated.

"Man, I'm telling you that Baby World is fire."

"We don't know." LR smiled. "You heard the old lady. This is the best she had in her life," he said.

"Ay man, our work here is done on that tip Nasty says arrogantly. We proved our point. Need we say more?" Nasty asked.

Baby J, Uno, Nasty, and LR walked to the front of the projects.

"Dig," Uno whispered. "Look down the block. You see the white SS?"

"Yeah, yeah."

"My little nigga King in there. He got a kilo in there for you. I'm leaving it here with you. Just pay me later. How's that for you?" Uno asked.

"Sound good," Baby J replied.

"Okay, I need you to make a call to your California people and tell them to send twenty men for me. I will pay for everything. I need to get this nigga Man-Man out the way. I was going to let him eat, but he's doing too much," Uno said as he, Nasty, and LR hopped in the Rolls.

Chapter 39

In just two weeks, the word had traveled like lightning. Niggas from outside counties were trying to get their hands on the Walking Dead.

King had finally given in. At first, he was only distributing the dope to his people. The more he refused to sell dope to the outsider, the more calls he got. He knew he had his hands on the best dope, and even with refusing everyone, it made them want it more. Since he knew that, he only sold to people he wanted to.

King passed a shopping bag over to his passenger. His passenger, in return, handed him a bag that consisted of $30,000. It was fucking King's head up that people were buying the dope at the price Uno had set. He heard all types of bitching, but in the end, they called him right back.

The man in the passenger seat was one of Reese's guys he'd met in prison a few years back. As soon as Reese touched down, he linked all of them with King.

"If shit hits right, I'm going to need three hundred more by the morning. If you have to, put it to the side for me because my spots been pumping nonstop," he said.

"I got you, all day," King replied.

The federal agents Rock and Grant stood around the office, watching a news clip on Rock's iPhone. Agent Rock's face was stone as he watched.

"Thirty-six shootings and murders in the last month," Agent Rock said as he shook his head. "We have never had this many murders and shootings in one month," he said as he looked at Agent Grant. "Ever since they stepped out, it's been a war out there on the streets. I will put my last dollar on it that they are behind all this. Silly motherfucker! We have to get them before everyone in the city is in the ground! We have to get them now!" he shouted as he tossed all his papers off his desk.

"But how we supposed to do that when we don't know if they behind what you're saying?" Agent Grant asked.

In Avon...

Uno and LR had just finished doing their workout. Each morning, they would work out for two hours. While they were locked up, they both kept up their bodies. They both knew that for them to keep up with what was going on around them, they had to keep their bodies and minds right.

They stood, sweating, drinking water while watching the news on TV. The reports were ranting on and on about the drastic increase in murders that were happening in the city.

Uno shook his head at what the report was saying. "Bro, you know, for us to survive out here, we have to move with the times. These young dudes can't think and have nothing to live for, so we have to go back to how we used to be. Ruthless," Uno said to LR. "I got a call from Desiree, and she clicked me in with the nigga Music," Uno said.

"Music? What for?" LR asked, looking at him crazily.

"He's the reason we know Jimmy was behind us getting locked up. But dig, he's coming to bring Man-Man a shipment in two weeks. My plan is to be ready to put our shit together. I'm trying to fly back with him. And bro, this whole time, I didn't know I had a son," Uno said, shaking his head.

"By who, and when?" LR asked.

"Long story, but by Jimmy's wife." He smiled.

"I can wait," LR said.

"Okay, well, one day, I went by their house to get that money he owed us when they stole that shipment. Well, she gave me a drink, and the next thing I know, she riding my dick, so that's when she had to get knocked, and that's the same reason Jimmy started playing us, but it's all good," Uno said.

Chapter 40

Snow walked toward the small, two-family house that sat right on the corner of 25th and Adams. Just as he reached the porch, he turned around to check his back. He spun back around, only to be greeted by Boo.

"Oh, shit!" Snow said.

"Don't move, or I will end your life now, homeboy," Boo said, grabbing Snow's .45 off his waist.

"Man, what's this about?" Snow asked.

Boo slapped him in the head, knocking him out cold. Lil' E came and helped him carry him to the truck, and they pulled off, followed by a car full of Boo's dudes.

Snow woke up in a dark room that smelled of death. It smelled of rotting flesh, shit, piss, sweat, blood, and dead bodies. It took his eyes some time to adjust to the darkness. He realized his hands and legs were chained. He was lying flat on a hard surface, and the bounds he had on were around his wrists and ankles, and he was spread-eagled.

"Hello!" Snow shouted, his voice echoing throughout the room. "Hello!" he said again, then the lights popped on.

Men were standing around the room, watching him. They all held a look of utter fear.

"I know what y'all want, but I had nothing to do with any of it!" Snow screamed.

"Of course you did!" LR said, smiling from ear to ear.

"Why you bring me here?" Snow asked.

"Because you're loyal. And goons like you don't talk unless you are encouraged to do so," LR told him.

"And you think just because you have me like this, you going to get what you're looking for. If that's your case, then you know loyal niggas like me don't break at all," Snow said.

LR laughed. "Everyone breaks, Snow. You might put up a good fight, but in the end, you will break. I promise that."

"That let's get this over with," Snow said, leaning his head back.

"I need to know all the information on Man-Man," LR told him.

Snow burst into laughter. "You better off killing me now because I can't bite the hand that feeds me," Snow said.

LR nodded at Boo. Snow discovered what the cables and wrenches were for. Boo started the generators, and the wenches popped on. Hitting the lever of the wrenches, and simultaneously, the chain that bound his wrists and ankles began to pull. Snow found himself being pulled in all types of directions. The pain became excruciating for him.

"Ahhh!" Snow cried out.

LR nodded at Boo, who cut the generators off. He then led in. "Give me what I want," he said into Snow's ear. Walking over to where LR stood, Lil' E looked down at Snow. Looking up, Snow knew his life was in their hands.

"Please, please. It hurt so bad," Snow said.

"You shot at me and got my little bro in a coma," Lil' E said, nodding at Boo, who turned the generators back on, pulling his limbs in further different directions, stretching his body in such ways that you could hear the popping sounds.

Nodding at Boo again, Lil' E looked down to see Snow shaking his head.

"Okay! Man-Man main spot is on East Street, and another spot is at 1426 English Avenue," Snow said.

"Now, how hard was that?" LR asked with a smile on his face. "I told you. Everyone breaks."

LR turned around and walked over to Uno and Nasty, who had been over in the dark corner the whole time. "We need to meet the plug and find these dudes and get to this money," LR said.

"Take that chump and do something with him," Lil' E said to Boo, following the rest out the door.

Later that night…

Sitting at the table were Uno, LR, Nasty, and Lil' E.

"We got men outside their spot on English Avenue," Boo said, walking into the room.

"Good," Nasty said.

"Sit. You part of the inner circle now. You have shown your loyalty, so here," Uno said, handing him a box.

Opening the box, Boo saw it was a bigger chin with WSF hanging from it.

"This means you're with the big boys now," Nasty said.

"Also, here." Uno placed the bag on the table.

Looking inside, Boo saw stacks of money and a brick of heroin.

Chapter 41

The downtown mall was packed with shoppers waiting to get the new Jordan Fives. King, Reese, and Lil' E walked in a small cluster. Each of them had their hands filled with bags. As soon as they came out of the mall, they crossed the street, and Lil' E stopped in front of Steak 'n Shake, where a few young dudes sold waters and other things.

"Lil' E, what's good?" one of the young dudes shouted as he ran over and dapped him. The other men greeted him the same way. Lil' E stood there, talking to the young dudes, as they looked at him like the boss he was. They respected him not only for putting his G down in the streets, but he always made sure to give them game anytime they saw him.

After chopping it up for a minute, he gave them all three hundred dollars apiece, then they walked off gracefully.

King, Reese, and Lil' E continued up the block, then made a right onto another almost empty block. They all rode in Lil' E's Mercedes-Benz, so they had to walk a half block to get to it.

Man-Man, Two-Tall, Leo, and Smash sat in a Cadillac Escalade. Two-Tall watched closely as King, Reese, and Lil' E walked casually. They were so heavily engaged in their conversation that they didn't even see them.

"Let's go," Two-Tall said as he stepped on the gas. They'd been out there for the past few hours, waiting patiently. Purely out of coincidence, Man-Man wanted to go down there to grab some shoes when Smash spotted Lil' E's Benz. They knew they had him, so they were going to sit until he came out, but when they spotted him and the other two, they all had miles on their faces. Smash flicked the safety off his seventeen-shot nine-millimeter. He grabbed hold of the lever on the side of the seat and lifted it. He braced himself against the seat as he pressed the window button.

"Go," Two-Tall said just as he got a few facts from the group. In seconds, the loud sound of gunfire ripped through the air, echoing throughout the entire downtown area.

Boc! Boc! Boc! Boc! Boc!

The bullets ended up hitting the car that the group was walking past. They all turned around with shock on their faces. They ducked low, using the car as a shield. In a second, all three had their guns drawn and firing away.

Bloc! Bloc! Bloc! Boc! Boc! Boc! Boom! Boom! Boom! was all that could be heard ringing off.

The Cadillac Escalade sped off while Smash continued firing away. The sound of gunshots stopped, but then the police sirens could be heard. They all quickly stood to their feet, looked around, then piled into the Benz, and Lil' E sped away. Rage filled their hearts. At that point, the only thing on their mind was some get back.

***

Just when everyone in the city counted Tezzy out, he pulled through. After a few hours, he awoke from a coma, confused. It wasn't until his girlfriend told him the details that he began to remember all that had taken place. He moved around a little because his whole body was sore from all the lying down he'd been doing. He was just sitting there, staring at the machines he was plugged into, waiting for his girlfriend to come back.

"How you doing today?" the young, beautiful, light-skinned nurse came in and asked.

"In pain," he replied. "I need something for it, please."

"I already know, so I got you. This will help you," she said, handing him a cup of water and two pills.

"What's these?" he asked.

"Percocets and Oxycontin," she replied.

Tezzy popped the pills and downed the water.

"I need to change your bandages, so I will be back in a hot second," she said, exiting the room.

Hours later...

The Lexus pulled up to the hospital and double-parked in front as Tezzy's nurse strutted toward the car. The driver, Leo, leaned back in his seat, smoking a blunt and talking on the phone.

"I hit you back," he said as the nurse got inside and greeted him with a kiss on the cheek. She leaned her head back and then sighed. "Long day?" he asked.

"Beyond. You know I put in an extra six hours," she said.

"Get that bag, baby," he said.

"You know it. But guess who my patient was today?" she asked.

"Who you talking about? Because I don't have time for the guessing game," Leo said.

"Well, it was Wezzy, Tezzy, whatever you call him," she said.

"Yeah, his name Tezzy," he said with hatred in his voice. "What about him, though?" he asked.

"Well, they have him on my list of patients, so I will be nursing him back to health."

Leo listened with his mouth open, really not believing that Tezzy just fell into his lap.

"Baby, please don't let anyone know, because I need my job, and my boss said someone paid to keep his mouth shut about him getting out of the coma."

"I got you, babe. No need to worry yourself. It's between me and you. But the next time you go into work, I want you to give the nigga one of those fentanyl pills I have at the crib, and I got $20,000 for you.

Chapter 42

Uno sat in the back room of the bar. In front of him sat his plug. The plug listened to every word Uno spoke.

"The work is good, but I want better this next go around," Uno said.

"Better?" the plug asked with attitude. "That material is great," he said with confidence.

"See, that's where the problem lays. You think I'm looking for great when I want the best in the country. It's been taking my people a month to shake ten thousand bricks. That doesn't sound right to me," Uno said.

"Ten thousand bricks in a month?" The man snarls. "And you sitting here complaining? Any other person would be happy even to move four thousand."

Uno stared directly into the plug's eyes. "I'm not any other person. I'm Uno, so I'm not satisfied. I have an entire city on my shoulders, and I'm trying to push the gas to the limit. I have a goal I set already, and that's moving at least thirty thousand bricks.

The plug looked at Uno like he was crazy. "You playing jokes with me? That's a lot of dope to move."

"Yeah, and there's a lot of money to be made that I need."

"I have other orders to fill, too," the plug said.

"If you stop playing and do the right thing, you can cut all that off and only deal with me. It's a lot of money to be made, and I'm not stopping until I get it all. The little work I'm getting now is kids' play. I was just sitting in the cell for months. The feds tried to take my life, so I'm going to show them that I'm always going to be number one in my city. I sat back, thinking and planning, and now it's time for me to bring all that planning to the table."

Ever since Uno started fucking with Pedro, he had put up close to $2.1 million. It was nothing like what he used to do, but it was something. Even Nasty and LR had put up the same. The first rip, Lil' E didn't put his money up, but the last go, he walked away with $1.1 million.

"My point's been made. I have two years to do what I'm trying to do, so the ball's in your court. After two years, I'm done," Uno said. "How long it's going to take you to get my order together?"

***

Sadness filled the air inside the church. The church was packed with people from all different walks of life, from kids to church folks, the law, and drug dealers. The drug dealers outnumbered everyone else. The church looked like a drug dealer's convention. Most of the people present had been desensitized to death because murder took place every day in their lives. That still didn't stop people from dropping a few tears. The love and respect the people had for Tezzy was quite evident.

Tezzy's body lay in the beautiful, gold coffin, dressed in a fine Gucci suit. A few of his many women friends were sprinkled around the room, displaying sorrow. The men who loved him were full of sorrow as well, but refused to believe he was gone.

Although an actual war was declared with Man-Man's team and WSF's team, they felt like they crossed the line and touched him. He fought hard to get out of a coma, and then he ended up dying because someone just so happened to put fentanyl in his system.

WSF knew Man-Man played a part in it, so they'd already put their plan together to get at them. If they couldn't get their hands on Man-Man and his team, Uno decided to get revenge on everybody who loved them.

***

The dark-red, late-model Nissan crept up the street. Inside the Nissan were Lil' E, Reese, and King. They cruised up the block as Lil' E looked around and saw a few people on the block. The time of day had everything to do with why the block was empty.

He slowed down as they approached the middle of the block, trying not to bring any attention to themselves. They took notice of three dudes standing around, with a few dope fiends in front of them. They felt great satisfaction, knowing that one of the dudes who shot at them happened to be in the car, along with the one who shot Tezzy.

Lil' E got the word that he was the one who opened the trap in the mornings. They were all sure it would be the best time to get at him. The fewer people out there meant fewer guns. The Nissan pulled up a little further down the block. Reese and King's windows were rolled down, and they sat on the edge of their seats with their weapons drawn.

The three young men looked at the Nissan, thinking it was a dope fiend. They were caught totally off guard.

The dope fiends took off in opposite directions as soon as their eyes fell on the guns which hung from the window. *Boc! Boc! Boc! Boc! Boom! Boom! Boom!* They both forced the doors open and jumped out, firing. *Boc! Boc! Boc! Boom! Boom! Boom!* Two of the three hit the ground from the shots as Smash took off in a sprint in the opposite direction.

Reese chased the young man down, firing aggressively behind him. *Boom! Boom! Boom! Boom!* After the third shot, Smash tumbled over, falling face-first into the ground. Reese picked up his pace to catch up with Smash. He fired two more shots at the back of his head. *Boom! Boom!* It caused it to open. He wasted no time getting back to the getaway car. On his way there, he watched as King stood over his prey, squeezing away. *Boc! Boc! Boc!*

"Let's go!" Lil' E shouted as Reese was getting into the car.

Lil' E's voice snapped King out of his zone. He quickly ran to the car, hopped in, and slammed the door shut. They sped off down the block successfully.

Game Over!

Chapter 43

The hotel lobby of The West Inn was packed with Baby J's men from LA. Altogether, there was a total of thirty men, young and old. The young clerk at the counter eyeballed the men, trying to find a familiar face because she believed they were rappers or basketball players.

Baby J and another man stood before the young clerk. "We need fifteen rooms. All fifteen must be on the top floor."

Just as the clerk was typing in the keys, Uno came and stepped through the automatic doors. He stepped up to the counter next to Baby J. They dapped hands and exchanged head nods.

Uno looked at the clerk. "How much is the total?"

"Altogether it'll be $2,565."

Uno pulled a hefty wad of hundreds from his pocket and counted out the total. He piled the stacks onto the counter.

"Sorry, sir. We only take credit cards; that way, we will have it on file," the clerk said, never once looking up at Uno.

Uno slapped another stack of bills on the counter. "That's fifteen hundred for you. We don't use credit cards."

"Okay," she said, finally looking into Uno's eyes.

She knew who Uno was, but she had never seen him in person before. She left and came back after a few minutes with a handful of keys and her manager.

"Welcome to The West Inn. If you need anything, and I mean anything, just hit us," the manager said, eyeballing Uno and Baby J.

Baby J gathered all the keys and began passing them out to his men. Then he and Uno stepped off to the side.

"So what's up, cuz?" Baby J asked.

"I have two different situations I need handled, like, in the next few days. One is in town, and another in New Mexico," Uno said.

"Well, let's get it over with," Baby J said with determination in his eyes.

Uno went into his pocket and handed Baby J a wad of cash.

"This is for whatever they need for now. Don't trip about anything. I got y'all covered. When I'm ready for them, I will call you," Uno said, walking off.

***

Uno cruised while listening to the tunes of Moneybagg Yo. The sound system was blazing loudly, so crisp and clear as if he was actually there with him. He pulled into the parking lot of Desiree's office building. He turned the music down from his steering wheel and pressed another button. He dialed Desiree's number and listened as it rang over the intercom. After a few rings, she picked up.

"What's happening, bro?" she asked casually.

"You tell me!" Uno barked in a demanding but joking manner. He pulled into the parking space right in the middle of Desiree's and Amayo's BMWs.

Uno looked up at Desiree's office window. "Look out the window," he demanded.

Desiree got up from her desk and walked over to the window.

"What's up?" she asked as she looked out of the window. What lay before her eyes was her dream car. She had to re-adjust her glasses, just to make sure she was actually seeing right. Her mouth popped open in awe as her eyes lay on the medallion. She recognized the mark instantly. It was a Rolls-Royce.

Uno sat behind the pitch-black-tinted windows with a smile on his face.

Desiree stood there, speechless. She had mixed feelings. She was happy for Uno, but at the same time, she was fearful. She knew it would be like a slap in the face to the feds.

"Come outside and talk to me," Uno demanded before hanging up.

As Uno waited for her to come out, he shuffled through his CDs. Just as Desiree was walking outside, she began shaking her head. By the time she was at the door, all that could be heard was Gangsta Boo's 'Can I Get Paid' playing.

She got in and slammed the heavy door shut. "This is a beautiful piece of art," she said, hiding how mad she was.

"Yeah... Art. You said it correct," he said with a grin.

"Uno, tell me you didn't go buy this," she said.

"I can't tell you that," he responded.

Desiree shook her head.

"Before you start trying to tell me what this would buying I'm vibing right now, so don't kill it for me," he said.

"Okay, I will hold my tongue," she said.

"I got something for you," he said, reaching into the back seat and grabbing a bag for her.

Desiree opened the bag to find a pair of $1,000 Proenza Schouler sandals, $400 Miu-Miu gold-plated Swarovski earrings, $355 Oliver Spencer sunglasses, and a $15,000 Cartier watch.

"Thank you!" she said, wiping her eyes.

"Naw, thank you for all the time you put in on our case. It's a bag for Amayo, also, back there," Uno said.

Hours later...

Uno slouched low as he cruised in the "Beast," as he called it. In the car with him sat King, who was in total awe.

"I see you done got your weight up nice," Uno said to him.

"Something like that, but I'm still chasing it so I can get one of those," King said.

"Fucking with me, you will get there. This what a half mill' feels like. You feel how soft these seats are," Uno whispered.

Everyone watched in amazement as the Rolls-Royce cruised through the city. The dark-tinted windows caused so much mystery that everybody who passed by snapped their heads. They had no clue who was riding behind the dark tints, but they would've loved to know.

King watched everybody from behind the tinted windows as they received the most attention. He would've loved to be seen in the car. Just sitting in the car made him want to grind all day and night.

"Them niggas that did that to Tezzy," King whispered. "It's over!"

Uno looked over at King with a stone face. "As they should be."

Chapter 44

Agents Rock and Grant sat in their parked car. It was midnight and dark outside. The only lights that could be seen were the lights inside the baby mansion they were sitting outside of. They'd been sitting on the block for the last few hours, watching to see what or who would come.

This $1.5-million, 7,000-square-foot home, surrounded by four acres of green land, belonged to Uno and Brezzy. The feds were aware of her because of the phone list Uno had and the video visits she set up every other day for him.

Agent Grant spoke. "One thing I know is he knows how to ball out."

"That's for sure," Agent Rock said as he continued to snap pictures.

They were trying to keep tabs on Uno to see what he did, when he left, and when he came back home. As they watched, a limo pulled up to the house. Then it started pouring rain.

***

Jimmy's wife stood before Uno and Brezzy, hair soaked as the heavens cried tears of retribution upon her. Her wet skin glistened under the moonlight, and her body started shaking from the chilly wind that settled into her bones. Her face was a face Uno hadn't seen in years. Rage, hurt, and betrayal caused a lump to form in his throat as they stood there, staring silently at one another.

Silence surrounded them. There was so much that needed to be said, but Uno couldn't find his voice. Looking into her eyes, he saw a woman who carried pain.

The world seemed to move in slow motion, and Uno couldn't help but think it was all a setup.

She stood, terrified as she waited for Uno to say something or react. She asked for help with her eyes as she looked at Brezzy. Butterflies fluttered in her stomach. Tears began to flow down her cheeks. The hatred she saw in Uno's eyes dissolved into hurt.

"Please speak," she whispered as she lowered her head. She was so full of regret that it hurt her stomach.

"This isn't happening," he whispered as he walked out onto the porch. He stopped so close to her that there wasn't any room between them.

She was afraid to breathe, afraid to move, afraid of what he was going to do to her.

"I'm sorry, Uno," she said.

Uno cleared his throat and took a step back from her. He moved to the side and extended his hand in welcome.

"Come inside," he said.

She took a deep breath and walked into the house behind Brezzy.

"There's so much we need to talk about," she began. Before she could finish her sentence, she felt the cold steel of a gun as Uno entered behind her.

Her body tensed, and she closed her eyes.

"I never meant to keep your son away, Uno," she said. Her voice was full of sorrow. "I don't deserve your forgiveness, but Jimmy made me stay away. Even if you pull the trigger, just know I loved you from the first time I saw you. We have a son that looks just like you, who Jimmy treats poorly, but I can't get him out without getting us killed," she said.

"You could have reached out in some way," Uno said.

"I just told you!" she said, raising her voice. She closed her eyes and composed herself, taking a deep breath. She had no right to raise her voice in his home. He was a victim of her betrayal.

"Take a shower and meet me down in the basement. We have a lot to talk about," he said.

She shook her head and retreated inside the room as he walked away toward Brezzy, who was in the kitchen, fixing tea.

Tears stung the lids of Savannah's eyes as she stood under the steaming hot water with her head hung low. The slight sound caused her to jump as she pulled back the shower curtain in a state of paranoia.

"Sorry if I scared you," Breezy said as she set the towel, lotion, and some underclothes on the sink.

"Thank you," Savannah said, stepping out, not caring that Brezzy still stood in the bathroom. She quickly dressed, throwing on the underclothes.

"He's downstairs, waiting on you," Breezy said, walking out.

Savannah hesitantly made her way down the stairs to meet Uno.

Uno stood at the bay window, watching the rain pour down. Although his back was facing the door, he immediately felt Savannah's presence when she walked into the room.

"Uno," she said with a hint of desperation in her tone, and in an instant, he was across the room, standing in her face.

"I want to know everything that he put you and my son through. I also need all the info I can use to get at him," he said.

"Okay, but look," she said, pulling a phone out and flicking through some pictures.

Uno stood there, looking at pictures of his son that looked just like him and Pooder. He had big legs like theirs. Seeing the pictures made him miss his daughter even more. He had his mother and daughter staying with his little sister down south.

"So how can I get in and get out?" Uno asked.

For the next twenty minutes, Savannah broke down all the ins and outs of the house. Jimmy had tunas under the house where Uno was going to have Music put some of his men. For the plan to work, Music's help was a must.

The agents continued to watch Uno's house from down the block. They were both leaning way back in their seats, eating donuts.

"This job takes patience and focus. I want him so bad. I will put all my time into this. It's nothing else for me to do," Agent Rock said.

Chapter 45

Uno sat comfortably on the huge bean bag as he removed stacks of money from a duffle bag that sat between his feet. He piled the money onto the floor. There was no way could he sit there and count $2 million. Reese told him the count was right, so he took him for his word.

The money came from the last shipment he just gave to his team, not even two weeks ago. Uno felt great that they moved the shipment half a week before they were supposed to.

Uno slid a few stacks of money to the side. The pile that was left, he put back into the duffle bag, putting the stack he slid to the side into another bag. He stood up and grabbed both bags. He put the bigger bag into a bedroom, which already had a few other bags in it.

He walked over to the huge window and stared over at the ocean in Miami. He absolutely loved the view. In fact, he loved everything about the building. Ant owned the building. It featured a private spa, health club, restaurant, gym, and track. It had all the amenities that one needs to live comfortably.

People would love to stay there, but Ant gave the apartment to him so he could stash his cash without any worries about anything or anyone. He knew from the feds that he had to put up for a rainy day. They'd locked up all of his accounts, and he didn't trust anyone with his money but his brother, because he knew he would take care of his kids for him if anything went wrong.

Back in Indianapolis...

The housing complex was packed with people. Dope dealers covered the whole complex as customers ran back and forth, getting their dope. All you heard was 'Walking Dead' being screamed.

On the outside of the complex, a tinted Cadillac Escalade pulled up to the entrance. Inside the truck, there sat Man-Man, Leo, and Two-Tall with heavy artillery. Leo peeked around, then picked up his phone and hit the chirp. "Where y'all at?" he asked into the phone.

A black Lincoln Navigator with tinted windows bent the corner. Leo's pups were in the vehicle. Each one of them held heavy artillery as well, with enough ammo. As the two vehicles sat in the middle of the block, talking, the lookouts from the complex noticed them and yelled out their code for danger.

Everyone stood at attention, and their focus was on the two trucks sitting outside the complex.

King and Reese studied the vehicles carefully, but as it was getting dark outside, and the tints were dark, they couldn't see inside. They both knew it was not looking right with them just sitting there.

King yelled a code, and in seconds, guns were drawn. Four men surrounded him and Reese as if they were Trump. Not only were they strapped, but every man in the complex had their own straps. The complex was guarded.

After Reese saw that everyone was in place, he stepped out with King beside him, and they both threw their hands in the air. Reese waved his hand for them to pull into the complex.

Man-Man sat back furiously. As bad as they should've gone in those, he knew it would've been silly. He hit his phone. "It's not the right time," he said into the phone. "Let's bounce outta here," he said before Leo pulled off.

They all realized how foolish it would have been to pull into the complex, but that would not stop them from carrying out their plan to get back at them. One way or another, they were sure they would get another chance to get at them.

"That was them niggas Man-Man and them," Reese said to King as they went back into grinding mode.

"Yeah, I know. When Uno pull up tomorrow, we got to holler at him because I'm not with all this back-and-forth shit. That's how we lost Drake and Ali in LA," King said.

Chapter 46

Agents Rock and Grant sat parked outside of Brick City Projects on the southside of the city. They had their eyes fixed on the traffic that went in and out of the projects. Watching the heavy activity infuriated them to no end.

"Look at this shit here," Agent Rock said with rage and fire. "I haven't seen this much activity since before the fuckers went in."

"Yeah?" Grant questioned. He didn't know what that looked like since he'd only been there for a short period of time.

"Yeah. Before we locked them up, the whole city looked like this. But the only thing is it was crack then, not heroin. At first, every kid on the block was only trying to get money for cars and clothes. It was murders, but this heroin is a whole different ball game. Our man and his crew corrupted this city, and they gave them a second time to do it again," Agent Rock says with disgust.

The projects were swarming with customers who were all in search of Walking Dead. Agent Rock and Grant's cameras were aimed at all the activities. They sat on the block, writing down license plates so they could get names and addresses.

It was a new day as he aimed the camera at the building in the middle where six dudes stood.

"Just look at these stupid motherfuckers," Agent Rock said as he snapped away with the camera as the WSF moved around.

Uno, LR, Nasty, Lil' E, Boo, Reese, and King stood in the middle of the commotion that was going on. They all watched the activity with great appreciation.

"Walking Dead! Walking Dead!" a young dealer shouted loudly for all to hear.

"Y'all hear that shit?" Uno asked, looking around. "Look at what we all have done in just months. And to think you didn't believe me, King. I told you we would set the tone around the city. We raising the bar. We putting life back into the city, and we started right here."

"You have to make sure everything is on the up and up out here. You say you trying to get back. Well, you and Reese have the keys to the city with Boo helping y'all. Me, Nasty, and Lil' E is good, so we going to let y'all do y'all. As long as y'all run this shit like a business, y'all will be able to have a long run," Uno said.

"Yeah, the only thing we need to get ahold of is the murders because that brings a whole new ball game. We understand we had to do what we had to do to pump life back, but now it's time to focus on the money," Nasty said.

"What about Man-Man and his team? Because they pulled up days ago but didn't come in. We have to get at them," King said.

"We going to handle that in a day or so," LR said.

"We about to have a shipment coming in here in the next day, so y'all will have about ten thousand bricks, and they all for y'all. Now, this where y'all should turn it all the way up. It took us too long the last time, but I have faith in y'all. Our goal is to move ten thousand every two weeks so, that way, we can stack up and enjoy life. We going to be going out of town to handle some important business, so y'all have to hold the city down," Uno said.

"Coo', coo'," Reese replied.

"Our plan is to make sure y'all have $1 million put up in a few weeks. We going to put all the money up for the shipment. Just give us our cut, and y'all split the rest between y'all and y'all team," Uno said.

Agent Rock snapped another series of shots of all the men smiling.

Chapter 47

Man-Man and Two-Tall were deep in the cut of the apartments. They sat on the green box as four of their men, equipped with pistols, surrounded them. They passed the blunt and bottle around, just smoking and joking around, passing the time. A fat boy walked fast toward Man-Man with a wad of cash. When he got to Man-Man, he handed it to him.

"That's another $1,000," he said before he began walking back toward the basketball court.

As Man-Man counted the wad of cash, a Mercedes Sprinter van cruised through the entrance. He paid no attention to the van; he just continued to count. When the second Sprinter van pulled into the complex, he looked up.

One van went toward the back, while the second one stopped in the middle. When both vans captured everyone's attention, it was too late. Baby J's men spilled from the vans, assault rifles and semi-automatics already firing. Twenty men spread out around the area, as if they were the police. Machine gunfire sounded off consecutively without a second in between. The element of surprise caught everybody off guard.

Instead of returning fire in their defense, they all ran for their lives. The men attempted to get away, but Baby J's men hawked them down one by one. Instead of firing to protect their boss or even themselves, they all took flight in different directions.

Man-Man stood in total shock at what was going on, not able to move. Fear had his body paralyzed in the same spot. He looked around, not seeing Two-Tall anywhere. Tears began to flow down his face. He peeked his head around the corner, using the building as a shield. His heart beat a mile a minute. After all the years of grinding in the streets, he had never seen anything like that before. It all happened so fast. He watched as his men were gunned down like animals being hunted.

He finally got the heart to move to save himself from being a captive. As he turned around and took a step, he faced his biggest nightmare. Uno and LR stood eye to eye with him. Uno snatched him by his jacket and shoved the .357 into his mouth. He gulped with fear.

"Finally," Uno said with a smile of satisfaction spreading across his face.

"Let's go," LR said, shoving him.

15 minutes later...

Uno looked down at Man-Man and slapped the shit out of him. "Wake your bitch ass up!"

Man-Man slowly opened his eyes, and fear showed all over his face upon seeing Uno, Nasty, LR, and Baby J standing around him.

"Just tell us where Jimmy stash houses are in Mexico, and you'll make it to see another day," LR said calmly.

Man-Man attempted to speak, but Uno smacked him, making him yelp in pain. "We ain't got all day! Talk, hoe ass nigga!"

When Man-Man didn't speak, LR started studying him. He guessed he didn't take them seriously. Man-Man looked at LR blankly, his eyes as rebellious as could be, and the look rubbed LR the wrong way. Suddenly, LR went into a blind fury. He wanted to smash his skull in.

"He's a tough guy. He ain't gonna talk until we make him talk. Ain't that right?" Uno asked, grabbing the knife Nasty had on the oven the whole time. "Strip this bitch," Uno said as Baby J and LR began pulling his clothes off.

Nasty punched him in the stomach, making him bend over in pain, and when he did, Uno stabbed the knife inside his asshole and twisted it.

"Mmmrrrpphh! Gggrrraaammpph!" His muffled screams could be heard throughout the house.

"Feel like talking now?" LR asked.

Man-Man nodded his head repeatedly. "I will talk," he said before passing out.

Chapter 48

Music lay in his bed next to one of his lady friends, just thinking about his life. Rick Ross's "I'm a boss" ringtone severed his train of thought. Music picked up his phone and saw that the caller was calling from somewhere in Indianapolis. For a second, he contemplated not answering the phone, but answered it anyway.

"Yeah, hello?"

"Fuck is up, homeboy?"

"Who dis?"

"Ay, Music, stop playing, nigga. It's me, Uno."

"I ain't got time for games. It's after ten, and the only Uno I know don't have this number and wouldn't be calling me in the first place."

"Nigga, it's me," Uno said.

"What's up, bro? Man, where you at?" Music asked, excited to hear his voice.

"'Round the way, putting this plan together. I need your help bad," Uno said.

"Talk to me," Music said, sitting up in bed so he could hear his every word.

"Well, I have a hold on that nigga Man-Man, so me and my team will be driving into your whereabouts, so I need help getting in and out at the same time," Uno said.

"Tell you what. Meet me at the Phan-Reynosa International Bridge because that's the only entry since y'all driving in. I have people there. Just get in line six and you'll be good. I will have everything ya need once you cross over, and a few of my men will be waiting on you," Music said, happy the day had finally come for Jimmy to meet his maker.

The next day...

"Why you have us out here?" Music asked the man who had driven across town to meet. Peter "Butter" Pan was the man to see when you needed any artillery. He'd been down with Jimmy for the last fifteen years.

Music knew Uno and his team would need some serious power if they planned to get back to the U.S.

"It's out the way, fella," Butter said as he left, looking up and down the block.

"We need some big-boy shit. Some knock-the-house-down type artillery. We tryna put some niggas in the ground," LR said.

"I got what y'all need then. I got shit fresh out the box. I got MP-40s, MP-5s, and MPK-5 submachine guns that fire fifty rounds before you have to change clips. I got M-16s, AK-47s, and AR-15s," Butter said.

"We want two of each," Uno said.

"We also want extra clips and ammo," LR said.

Butter went into the building and came walking out ten minutes later with a black duffle bag. "Y'all got the money?" Butter asked.

"I got the money, big dog," Uno replied and tossed his own duffle bag over.

Butter, in turn, tossed his duffle bag at Uno's feet.

Uno picked up the bag and peered inside. Satisfied that everything was there, he thanked Butter, and they turned to leave.

"Hold on for a minute, Music and LR. I just thought about something."

Then Uno stopped and called out to Butter.

"What's up, young folks?"

"Is it true what they say?"

"Is what true?" Butter replied.

"What they say about you..."

Butter smiled. "What they say about me?"

"That you and Jimmy been fucking each other for years."

"Of course not. Niggas just be talking," Butter replied.

Uno upped his gun and fired three holes into his head, watching Butter's body drop.

"Get that money, LR, and come on."

Chapter 49

"LR, Lil' E, and Boo, y'all go find my baby and get her the hell out of New Mexico. Music said she's in the basement, but y'all have to go through the kitchen. Me and Nasty gon' grab the nigga. The ultimate goal is to get my family back to Indianapolis. Savannah will grab my son and go back with y'all. Under no circumstances do we leave without my family. If there's any surprises, y'all know what to do, right?" Uno asked.

"Let's get it then," LR said.

When Jimmy heard voices in his ear, he thought it was Savannah playing games, trying to wake him up, so he paid it no mind. Then came the hard slap across his face. Jimmy opened his eyes immediately.

"What the hell?" Then he felt himself being tossed to the floor. Under the bed, he saw the handgun he kept there, but thought against trying to grab it. The voice in his ear said, "Lay flat on your stomach, and don't move."

Uno waited until Jimmy complied before he continued. "You already know what time it is. We want the bread and whatever else you got in here. I know you got it here somewhere. Gimme that shit, and then we out," Uno said, watching Savannah grab her bag that was already packed.

"In that drawer over there by the wall, there's a little over two hundred gr—"

"Two hundred grand? Cut the bullshit. Your watch cost more than that. I know you got a safe in here somewhere."

"I don't … have no … safe. All the money is across the seas."

"Where the drugs at then?"

"Waiting on the shipment."

Uno smacked Jimmy again with the gun. He was in no mood for games.

Bloc! Bloc! Uno shot him in the hand.

"Okay, okay. I'll take you to the money! I'll take you to it!" Jimmy said, which sounded like music to their ears.

They lifted Jimmy up to his feet, and he stared at the last person he thought he would see. Uno wore a smile that made Jimmy's cheeks red, pushing him down the stairs and out the front door to the awaiting van that Music sat in.

"Music, you backstabber. When my peoples find out you had something to do with this, your whole family would be wiped off this earth," Jimmy said.

Smack. "Shut the fuck up," Uno said.

Jimmy gave Music the directions, and they ended up at a warehouse that had seen better days. Uno looked at him strangely as Jimmy revealed that the money was buried there.

"If you want to see another day, go dig it up," Uno said, getting out of the van.

"Need a shovel. And did you forget you just shot me in one of my hands?" Jimmy asked, holding his hand up.

They took the walk that led to the hidden treasure, while Music went to find a shovel.

A few minutes later, Music walked up to Jimmy and cut off the rip cuffs, then passed him one of the three shovels.

"Start digging," Uno said as he kicked him in the ass.

When Jimmy started trying to shovel the dirt with one hand, Uno shot him in the knee, grabbed the shovel, and began to help Nasty and Music. After close to thirty minutes of digging and sweating profusely, they thought he was playing.

"You want to play games?" Nasty asked, dropping the shovel.

"How? I swear it's a little more, and you will see," Jimmy said, scared to death.

Drenched in sweat, they began digging again until one of them hit something steel. Moving the rest of the dirt from the spot, they saw three waist-high steel safes. When they cleared away the rest of the dirt, Uno tried to open one but failed. He then used the shovel, and it popped open. When they looked inside, they saw the safe was filled to the brim with thick, clear packets of old hundred-dollar bills.

"H-how much money is all this?" Nasty stammered, still shocked by the fortune they'd just dug up.

"All the cash I have to my name is $25 million," he said, swallowing hard.

Frustrated, Uno smacked the taste out of Jimmy's mouth.

"P-please don't kill me. I'll just leave, and you will never see me again. I swear to God," he begged. "Wait! I got mo—"

Uno raised his gun and shot Jimmy in the forehead.

When he glanced up after smoking Jimmy, Music and Nasty looked at Uno with grins on their faces. By the time they removed all the money and close to a hundred kilos of dope, darkness had covered the city.

They sped back to the hotel they were staying in, not believing the lick they'd just pulled off. They transported all the cash and drugs. Uno never knew one man could have so much money in the ground.

By the time they broke bread, his cell phone had rang several times.

When they got up to leave, Music hugged both Uno and Nasty.

"I appreciate this, for real, y'all," Music said.

"Shit, we appreciate you for getting him and saving my family," Uno said.

Chapter 50

"Hello?" The voice sounded as though it were crying and distraught, but Uno still recognized it.

"Baby!" he yelled. "Baby! Where you at?" he asked.

"Baby... I'm safe. I'm at Nasty's club," she said.

"I'm on my way," Uno said, attitude changing in seconds from worry and fear to happiness and hope.

"No! No, you can't," she blurted out. She quickly informed him about the FBI agents coming to the club to look for him, Nasty, Lil' E, and LR with warrants for their arrest.

"Damn!" Uno said.

"LR said meet him at the pink house," she said.

"Okay, I love you, baby," he said before hanging up.

"We fucked up big time, bro," Uno said, looking at Nasty as they sped through the checkpoint.

"What's up?" Nasty asked.

"The FBI agents was in the club looking for us, but LR told us to meet him at the pink house."

Wanting to see his baby so bad, Uno knew the police were going to stop them for speeding. His eyes were glued to the rearview mirror as soon as they made it back safely in the U.S. Although his family was safe, he was still alert because of the FBI. They made it to the pink house in record time, and Uno bolted from the car as Nasty went to get breakfast.

Uno unlocked the door, and as soon as he walked into the house, a ferocious and surprising blow rocked his body. He tried to recover from the drunken wooziness that consumed him, but the two figures hit him again at the same time. He dropped instantly.

Looking around, Uno saw LR's body lying out. Then he noticed the huge man towering over his body. When the light in the room came on, Uno saw the fed dude who had been at every one of his past court dates.

Seconds later, Uno heard a voice that was imprinted in his brain. Brezzy's frame appeared before his eyes. She held a black .380 in her hand that Uno had given her a month prior.

'How could I be so fucking silly?' he thought, not believing the woman he was ready to marry and kill with had led him into a trap. Uno was glad Nasty went to get breakfast.

Hitting the chirp button on his phone, which was inside his pocket, he held it down so Nasty could hear everything.

"Bitch, I'm going to kill you," LR said, waking up.

Brezzy laughed at him. "I been waiting a long time for this day to come," she said.

"You hear me, bitch?" LR yelled.

Boc! Boc! Boc! She hit LR all in the chest.

Years Earlier...

Breezy was off in college when she got the devastating news of her parents' deaths. Although she understood the promise of death, she couldn't accept it when it came to them.

Days after burying her parents, she went to their house on Eugene and discovered that they had video cameras installed outside and throughout the house. She searched room after room until she found a secret room that had TVs and videos stacked. She sat in that house for days, going through hours of video, until she came across a video that showed LR grabbing something or putting it back.

Her father walked up to him from the back, but when LR turned around, he ended up stabbing her father in the neck, which made him drop the gun in his hand and reach for his neck. Then she saw LR shoot. A minute later, Uno came running from the front and pushed LR toward the front. She then watched Nasty having a few people pick up the body and lay it in the backyard. Then they went into the house and shot her mother six times.

Instead of going to the police, she went to her cousin, who was a fed, and together, their cunning minds began formulating a secretive and solid plan for WSF's demise. In their constant relationship, Breezy hated masking her true feelings. It reminded her that she was sleeping with the enemy.

This bitch was definitely the master of the game. She was good. "Fuck it, Brezzy! Just go for what you know because you already know I'm not going to sit here and beg for my life," Uno said.

"Don't trip. We'll get to everything that you want in due time, but right now, you on my time," she said.

"Well, bitch, we were behind your parents getting killed. What you going to do about it? I have done shit in my life niggas wish they could. My family will be taken care of for the rest of their lives, so I'm good," Uno said.

"I loved my parents, and you took them from me, so I'm going to take you from your kids, honey," she said.

Nasty sat there, listening to everything that was going on in the house, and the stuff was messing with his head. He made a U-turn as soon as he heard them talking. He texted Lil' E on his other phone and told him to meet him at the pink house with a few guns since they came straight there from Mexico. Both Nasty and Lil' E pulled onto the block at the same time.

"Let's go through the back door," Lil' E said, leading the way.

Walking through the back door, they stood in the kitchen, listening to Brezzy cry and talk about her parents. Nasty peeked around the corner and made eye contact with Uno.

The fed stood off to the side, leaning against the wall, typing away on his phone.

"I take Brezzy, and you take the Fed," Nasty whispered.

When Uno saw Nasty, he looked up and smiled at Brezzy.

"You know one thing about me, Breezy?" Uno asked.

"What?" she responded.

"Today isn't my day, but as you have me on my knees like I'm a bitch, I wondered if you and that fed over there ever think today would be y'all's day?" Uno asked just as Lil' E walked up on the fed.

Boc! Boc! Lil' E pulled the trigger, hitting the fed all in the head.

Breezy spun around but was slapped by Nasty's gun, which knocked her out cold.

Uno got up and rushed to check LR to make sure he was okay. "Lil' E, I need you to get him to the family doc," he said, helping pick LR's body up and take him to the car.

When Uno walked back into the house, Nasty already had Brezzy on her knees and begging for her life.

"You know you fucked up, right?" Uno asked, picking up her .380 and placing it in her mouth. "I want you to look into my eyes before I kill you," he said.

Boc! Boc! Boc! He shot into her mouth.

Uno and Nasty walked out of the house, heading to the car so they could meet up with Lil' E and LR at the doc's house.

"It took a lot to get here, bro, but we made it, my nigga. Now, all we have to do is get these warrants off us, so first thing, I'm going to get Desiree on it," Uno said.

As they talked, they saw LR's green Audi pulling up on the block. Punkin jumped out and ran into Uno's arms.

"Baby, I missed you so much," she said, crying her eyes out.

"It's all over with, baby," Uno said, watching Savannah and a boy get out of the car as well.

"Come on, y'all," Punkin said, waving Savannah and the young boy over.

Savannah came into the circle and hugged him tight.

"Now, can we all be a family and have fun?" Savannah asked, beginning to cry, too. "Jarimiah, come say hello to your father," Savannah said, looking at the young boy.

"I'm okay, Mom," he said back.

"Jarimiah Omar-Anthony Brandon, if you don't bring your little butt here and say hello, I'm going to break this heel off in our ass," Savannah said, turning red.

"We have enough time for all that. Let's get out of here. We have too much money in the car and bodies in the house," Uno said, pushing them toward their car as he sat in Nasty's.

Epilogue

One week later, Brezzy's going-home service was at a little church on the east side of Indianapolis. The church was filled with police officers, family members, and people from the streets, Uno reckoned. He didn't understand how so many people could find out that she'd been working with the feds and still came out to show love. Everyone looked sad and somber while viewing Brezzy's body, which lay in a pink pearl casket sitting in front of the whole church.

Sitting behind a fake wig and dark glasses, Uno looked at Brezzy's face with mixed feelings. Punkin and Savannah were there to support him since they knew she was due to have his baby. Although he knew they had gotten away clear with both murders, Uno knew deep down that one day, death would come knocking at their door.

Killing Agent Rock hurt because, before he had gone off to the pink house, he had given some pictures and other things to his boss that put a spotlight on WSF.

Days before Brezzy's death, she went out with Uno, and to show him she loved him, they went to her lawyer's office and had his name added to all her paperwork. In the end, Uno received the biggest blessing.

THE END

Lock Down Publications and Ca$h Presents
Assisted Publishing Packages

Due to an increase in the price of services we have increased our prices. The prices below reflect the price increase as of 11/1/24.

BASIC PACKAGE $699 Editing Cover Design Formatting	UPGRADED PACKAGE $1000 Typing Editing Cover Design Formatting Upload eBooks to Amazon Upload Paperback to Amazon
ADVANCE PACKAGE $1,400 Typing Editing (line editing/content) Cover Design Formatting Copyright Registration Proofreading Upload eBooks to Amazon Upload Paperback to Amazon	LDP SUPREME PACKAGE $1,700 Typing Editing (line editing/content) Cover Design Formatting Copyright Registration Proofreading Set up Amazon Account Upload eBooks to Amazon Upload Paperback to Amazon Advertise on LDP's Amazon and Facebook Page

***

Other services available upon request.
Additional charges may apply

Lock Down Publications
P.O. Box 944
Stockbridge, GA 30281-9998
Phone: 470 303-9761
Email: lockdownpublications@gmail.com

Submission Guideline

Submit the first three chapters of your completed manuscript to ldpsubmissions@gmail.com. In the subject line add **Your Book's Title**. The manuscript must be in a Word Doc file and sent as an attachment. Document should be in Times New Roman, double spaced, and in size 12 font. Also, provide your synopsis and full contact information. If sending multiple submissions, they must each be in a separate email.

Have a story but no way to send it electronically? You can still submit to LDP/Ca$h Presents. Send in the first three chapters, written or typed, of your completed manuscript to:

LDP: Submissions Dept
P.O. Box 944
Stockbridge, GA 30281-9998

DO NOT send original manuscript. Must be a duplicate. Provide your synopsis and a cover letter containing your full contact information.

Thanks for considering LDP and Ca$h Presents.

NEW RELEASES

BLOODLINE OF A SAVAGE 1-3
THESE VICIOUS STREETS 1-3
RELENTLESS GOON 1-3
BY PRINCE A. TAUHID

THE BUTTERFLY MAFIA 1-3
BY FUMIYA PAYNE

A THUG'S STREET PRINCESS 1&2
BY MEESHA

CITY OF SMOKE 3
BY MOLOTTI

GET IT IN SLUGS 1 &2
BY B. STALL

STANDING ON HER BUSINESS 1&2
BY DG SANTANA

STEPPERS 1,2&3
THE REAL BADDIES OF CHI-RAQ
BY KING RIO

THE LANE 1&2
BY KEN-KEN SPENCE

THUG OF SPADES 1&2
LOVE IN THE TRENCHES 2
CORNER BOYS
BY COREY ROBINSON

TIL DEATH 3
BY ARYANNA

THE BIRTH OF A GANGSTER 4
BY DELMONT PLAYER

PRODUCT OF THE STREETS 1-3
BY DEMOND "MONEY" ANDERSON

NO TIME FOR ERROR
BY KEESE

MONEY HUNGRY DEMONS 1-2
BY TRANAY ADAMS

HUB CITY MENACE 1-3
BY J. WHITE

A THUGGISH PASSION 1&2
LAND OF DA HOOLIGANZ 1-4
KILLAZ ON STANDBY 1&2
BY IRA B.

FO'EVA ROLLIN 1&2
BY ASSA RAYMOND BAKER

THE LEVEL UP 1&3
BY LUXURY KING

Coming Soon from Lock Down Publications/Ca$h Presents

IF YOU CROSS ME ONCE 6
ANGEL V
By Anthony Fields

A THUGS STREET PRINCESS 3
By Meesha

CORNER BOYS 2
By Corey Robinson

THA TAKEOVER
By Keith Chandler

BETRAYAL OF A G 2
By Ray Vinci

SAVAGE FAMILY EMPIRE 1&2
SOULLESS GOON 1,2&3
THE DIRTY SIDE OF MONEY 1,2&3
By Prince

FOR MY ENEMY'S SAKE
AMBITIONS OF A SLIDER
FRESH OFF DA PORCH
By IRA B.

BY THE TRUCKLOAD 1-4
TIPPIN' THE SCALES 1-3
BAD BITCHES WIT GUNZ 3
PROBLEM SOLVED 2
By Christopher "Diesel" Hornezes

Available Now

RESTRAINING ORDER 1 & 2
By **CA$H & Coffee**

LOVE KNOWS NO BOUNDARIES 1-3
By **Coffee**

RAISED AS A GOON I, II, III & IV
BRED BY THE SLUMS I, II, III
BLAST FOR ME I & II
ROTTEN TO THE CORE I II III
A BRONX TALE I, II, III
DUFFLE BAG CARTEL I II III IV V VI
HEARTLESS GOON I II III IV V
A SAVAGE DOPEBOY I II
DRUG LORDS I II III
CUTTHROAT MAFIA I II
KING OF THE TRENCHES
By **Ghost**

LAY IT DOWN I & II
LAST OF A DYING BREED I II
BLOOD STAINS OF A SHOTTA I & II III
By **Jamaica**

LOYAL TO THE GAME I II III
LIFE OF SIN I, II III
By **TJ & Jelissa**

IF LOVING HIM IS WRONG…I & II
LOVE ME EVEN WHEN IT HURTS I II III
By **Jelissa**

PUSH IT TO THE LIMIT
By **Bre' Hayes**

THA TAKEOVER 3 | KEITH CHANDLER

BLOOD OF A BOSS 1-5
SHADOWS OF THE GAME
TRAP BASTARD
By **Askari**

THE STREETS BLEED MURDER 1-3
THE HEART OF A GANGSTA 1-3
By **Jerry Jackson**

WHEN A GOOD GIRL GOES BAD
By **Adrienne**

THE COST OF LOYALTY 1-3
By **Kweli**

BRIDE OF A HUSTLA 1-3
THE FETTI GIRLS 1-3
CORRUPTED BY A GANGSTA 1-4
BLINDED BY HIS LOVE
THE PRICE YOU PAY FOR LOVE 1-3
DOPE GIRL MAGIC 1-3
By **Destiny Skai**

A KINGPIN'S AMBITION
A KINGPIN'S AMBITION II
I MURDER FOR THE DOUGH
By **Ambitious**

TRUE SAVAGE 1-7
DOPE BOY MAGIC 1-3
MIDNIGHT CARTEL 1-3
CITY OF KINGZ 1&2
NIGHTMARE ON SILENT AVE
THE PLUG OF LIL MEXICO 1&2
CLASSIC CITY
By **Chris Green**

A GANGSTER'S REVENGE 1-4
THE BOSS MAN'S DAUGHTERS 1-5
A SAVAGE LOVE 1&2
BAE BELONGS TO ME 1&2
A HUSTLER'S DECEIT 1-3
WHAT BAD BITCHES DO 1-3
SOUL OF A MONSTER 1-3
KILL ZONE
A DOPE BOY'S QUEEN 1-3
TIL DEATH 1-3
IMMA DIE BOUT MINE 1-6
DYING FOR LIKES
By **Aryanna**

A DOPEBOY'S PRAYER
By **Eddie "Wolf" Lee**

THE KING CARTEL 1-3
By **Frank Gresham**

THESE NIGGAS AIN'T LOYAL 1-3
By **Nikki Tee**

GANGSTA SHYT 1-3
By **CATO**

THE ULTIMATE BETRAYAL
By **Phoenix**

BOSS'N UP 1-3
By **Royal Nicole**

I LOVE YOU TO DEATH
By **Destiny J**

I RIDE FOR MY HITTA
I STILL RIDE FOR MY HITTA
By **Misty Holt**

LOVE & CHASIN' PAPER
By **Qay Crockett**

TO DIE IN VAIN
SINS OF A HUSTLA
By **ASAD**

BROOKLYN HUSTLAZ
By **Boogsy Morina**

BROOKLYN ON LOCK 1 & 2
By **Sonovia**

GANGSTA CITY
By **Teddy Duke**

A DRUG KING AND HIS DIAMOND 1-3
A DOPEMAN'S RICHES
HER MAN, MINE'S TOO 1&2
CASH MONEY HO'S
THE WIFEY I USED TO BE 1&2
PRETTY GIRLS DO NASTY THINGS
By **Nicole Goosby**

LIPSTICK KILLAH 1-3
CRIME OF PASSION 1-3
FRIEND OR FOE 1-3
By **Mimi**

TRAPHOUSE KING 1-3
KINGPIN KILLAZ 1-3
STREET KINGS 1&2
PAID IN BLOOD 1&2
CARTEL KILLAZ 1-3
DOPE GODS 1&2
By **Hood Rich**

THE STREETS ARE CALLING
By **Duquie Wilson**

STEADY MOBBN' 1-3
THE STREETS STAINED MY SOUL 1-3
By **Marcellus Allen**

WHO SHOT YA 1-3
SON OF A DOPE FIEND 1-4
HEAVEN GOT A GHETTO 1&2
SKI MASK MONEY 1&2
By **Renta**

GORILLAZ IN THE BAY 1-4
TEARS OF A GANGSTA 1/&2
3X KRAZY 1&2
STRAIGHT BEAST MODE 1&2
By **DE'KARI**

TRIGGADALE 1-3
MURDA WAS THE CASE 1-3
By **Elijah R. Freeman**

SLAUGHTER GANG 1-3
RUTHLESS HEART 1-3
By **Willie Slaughter**

GOD BLESS THE TRAPPERS 1-3
THESE SCANDALOUS STREETS 1-3
FEAR MY GANGSTA 1-5
THESE STREETS DON'T LOVE NOBODY 1-2
BURY ME A G 1-5
A GANGSTA'S EMPIRE 1-4
THE DOPEMAN'S BODYGAURD 1&2
THE REALEST KILLAZ 1-3
THE LAST OF THE OGS 1-3
By **Tranay Adams**

MARRIED TO A BOSS 1-3
By **Destiny Skai & Chris Green**

KINGZ OF THE GAME 1-7
CRIME BOSS 1-4
By **Playa Ray**

FUK SHYT
By **Blakk Diamond**

DON'T F#CK WITH MY HEART 1&2
By **Linnea**

ADDICTED TO THE DRAMA 1-3
IN THE ARM OF HIS BOSS
By **Jamila**

LOYALTY AIN'T PROMISED 1&2
By **Keith Williams**

YAYO 1-4
A SHOOTER'S AMBITION 1&2
BRED IN THE GAME
By **S. Allen**

TRAP GOD 1-3
RICH $AVAGE 1-3
MONEY IN THE GRAVE 1-3
CARTEL MONEY 1&2
By **Martell Troublesome Bolden**

FOREVER GANGSTA 1&2
GLOCKS ON SATIN SHEETS 1&2
By **Adrian Dulan**

TOE TAGZ 1-4
LEVELS TO THIS SHYT 1&2
IT'S JUST ME AND YOU
By **Ah'Million**

KINGPIN DREAMS 1-3
RAN OFF ON DA PLUG
By **Paper Boi Rari**

THE STREETS MADE ME 1-3
By **Larry D. Wright**

CONFESSIONS OF A GANGSTA 1-4
CONFESSIONS OF A JACKBOY 1-3
CONFESSIONS OF A HITMAN
CONFESSIONS OF A DOPE BOY
By **Nicholas Lock**

I'M NOTHING WITHOUT HIS LOVE
SINS OF A THUG
TO THE THUG I LOVED BEFORE
A GANGSTA SAVED XMAS
IN A HUSTLER I TRUST
By **Monet Dragun**

QUIET MONEY 1-3
THUG LIFE 1-3
EXTENDED CLIP 1&2
A GANGSTA'S PARADISE
By **Trai'Quan**

CAUGHT UP IN THE LIFE 1-3
THE STREETS NEVER LET GO 1-3
By **Robert Baptiste**

NEW TO THE GAME 1-3
MONEY, MURDER & MEMORIES 1-3
By **Malik D. Rice**

CREAM 2-3
THE STREETS WILL TALK
By **Yolanda Moore**

THE STREETS WILL NEVER CLOSE 1-3
By **K'ajji**

LIFE OF A SAVAGE 1-4
A GANGSTA'S QUR'AN 1-4
MURDA SEASON 1-3
GANGLAND CARTEL 1-3
CHI'RAQ GANGSTAS 1-4
KILLERS ON ELM STREET 1-3
JACK BOYZ N DA BRONX 1-3
A DOPEBOY'S DREAM 1-3
JACK BOYS VS DOPE BOYS 1-3
COKE GIRLZ
COKE BOYS
SOSA GANG 1&2
BRONX SAVAGES
BODYMORE KINGPINS
BLOOD OF A GOON
By **Romell Tukes**

CONCRETE KILLA 1-3
VICIOUS LOYALTY 1-3
BLOODY MONEY BAGS
By **Kingpen**

THE ULTIMATE SACRIFICE 1-6
KHADIFI
IF YOU CROSS ME ONCE 1-3
ANGEL 1-4
IN THE BLINK OF AN EYE
By **Anthony Fields**

THE LIFE OF A HOOD STAR
By **Ca$h & Rashia Wilson**

NIGHTMARES OF A HUSTLA 1-3
BLOOD AND GAMES 1&2
By **King Dream**

GHOST MOB
By **Stilloan Robinson**

HARD AND RUTHLESS 1&2
MOB TOWN 251
THE BILLIONAIRE BENTLEYS 1-3
REAL G'S MOVE IN SILENCE
By **Von Diesel**

MOB TIES 1-7
SOUL OF A HUSTLER, HEART OF A KILLER 1-3
GORILLAZ IN THE TRENCHES
OOPS CRY TOO 1&2
THE DAUGHTER OF A CARTEL BOSS
By **SayNoMore**

BODYMORE MURDERLAND 1-3
THE BIRTH OF A GANGSTER 1-4
By **Delmont Player**

FOR THE LOVE OF A BOSS 1&2
By **C. D. Blue**

KILLA KOUNTY 1-5
TENDER
By **Khufu**

MOBBED UP 1-4
THE BRICK MAN 1-5
THE COCAINE PRINCESS 1-10
STEPPERS 1-3
SUPER GREMLIN 1-4
A GANGSTA'S SON
By **King Rio**

MONEY GAME 1&2
By **Smoove Dolla**

A GANGSTA'S KARMA 1-5
By **FLAME**

KING OF THE TRENCHES 1-3
By **GHOST & TRANAY ADAMS**

BAD BITCHES WIT GUNZ 1&2
PROBLEM SOLVED
By **"Christopher Diesel" Hornezes**

QUEEN OF THE ZOO 1&2
By **Black Migo**

GRIMEY WAYS 1-3
BETRAYAL OF A G
By **Ray Vinci**

XMAS WITH AN ATL SHOOTER
By **Ca$h & Destiny Skai**

KING KILLA 1&2
By **Vincent "Vitto" Holloway**

BETRAYAL OF A THUG 1&2
By **Fre$h**

COUNTDOWN OF A KILLA 1&2
SEX, MURDER AND GOD 1&2
GUNS DOWN, BOTTOMS UP 1&2
By Lo-Life

THE MURDER QUEENS 1-7
By **Michael Gallon**

FOR THE LOVE OF BLOOD 1-4
By **Jamel Mitchell**

HOOD CONSIGLIERE 1&2
NO TIME FOR ERROR
By **Keese**

PROTÉGÉ OF A LEGEND 1,2&3
LOVE IN THE TRENCHES 1&2
By **Corey Robinson**

THE PLUG'S RUTHLESS DAUGHTER 1&2
By **Tony Daniels**

BORN IN THE GRAVE 1-3
CRIME PAYS
By **Self Made Tay**

MOAN IN MY MOUTH
By **XTASY**

TORN BETWEEN A GANGSTER AND A GENTLEMAN
By **J-BLUNT & Miss Kim**

LOYALTY IS EVERYTHING 1-3
CITY OF SMOKE 1-3
By **Molotti**

HERE TODAY GONE TOMORROW 1&2
By **Fly Rock**

WOMEN LIE MEN LIE 1-4
FIFTY SHADES OF SNOW 1-3
STACK BEFORE YOU SPLURGE
GIRLS FALL LIKE DOMINOES
NAÏVE TO THE STREETS
By **ROY MILLIGAN**

PILLOW PRINCESS
By **S. Hawkins**

THE BUTTERFLY MAFIA 1-3
SALUTE MY SAVAGERY 1&2
By **Fumiya Payne**

THE LANE 1&2
By Ken-Ken Spence

THE PUSSY TRAP 1-5
By **Nene Capri**

DIRTY DNA
By **Blaque**

SANCTIFIED AND HORNY
by **XTASY**

BOOKS BY LDP'S CEO, CA$H

TRUST IN NO MAN
TRUST IN NO MAN 2
TRUST IN NO MAN 3
BONDED BY BLOOD
SHORTY GOT A THUG
THUGS CRY
THUGS CRY 2
THUGS CRY 3
TRUST NO BITCH
TRUST NO BITCH 2
TRUST NO BITCH 3
TIL MY CASKET DROPS
RESTRAINING ORDER
RESTRAINING ORDER 2
IN LOVE WITH A CONVICT
LIFE OF A HOOD STAR
XMAS WITH AN ATL SHOOTER